My Bedtime Book of
Magic Carpet Stories
from many Lands

PATRICIA TAYLOR

Illustrations by Tony Escott
Claude Kaïler and Rosemary Lowndes

WARD LOCK LIMITED

LONDON AND SYDNEY

Contents

Fatima and Shamsuzzakir found a magic carpet in a cave. It was the most wonderful carpet, for it took them everywhere in the world —from Afghanistan to Zambia. They met children and animals from every part of the world, they learned something about every country they visited, and they had more fun than any two children ever had before.

All the magic carpet stories are in this book. There are stories about all kinds of

and about all kinds of

so hop aboard the magic carpet!

Copyright © Eurobook Limited, 1970
Designed and produced for the Publisher
by Eurobook Limited, London

Hardbound edition with jacket
ISBN 7063 1290 2

Edition with picture boards
ISBN 7063 1289 9

Printed in Holland by N.O.I., Amsterdam.

The Magic Carpet

High in the cold, old Hindu Kush mountains of Afghanistan there was a man who lived all alone except for his flock of sheep. No one ever visited him, but he wasn't lonely. For the old man was making a magic carpet.

Now everyone knows that in Afghanistan they make truly beautiful and wonderful carpets. But only one of them ever was or ever will be a magic carpet. This is its story.

Every year the old man would shear the wool from his sheep. He spun it into thread, and he dyed it in many beautiful colours. Then he would take all the wool to his loom. There he sat, and closed his eyes, and dreamed. And as he dreamed, his hands

8

moved over the loom, weaving the wool into pictures of his dreams.

His dreams were magic dreams, for what he saw was real—real people and real things in real places all over the world. They were dreams of things that had happened a long time before, and that hadn't happened yet.

Many years he sat there, dreaming and weaving his wonderful pictures, until at last the carpet was done. Then he had one more dream. It was about himself, and what he would do with the carpet, and what would happen to it.

When the old man woke from his last dream, he smiled happily to himself. He picked up the beautiful magic carpet, and carried it to a cave high up on a mountain. There he hid the carpet, and went away, and never came back again.

Many years later a boy named Shamsuzzakir and his sister, Fatima, came to the cave. It was winter time, and very cold, and they were lost in a snow storm. They were very happy to find the cave, and even happier when they found the carpet. They sat down on it, and wrapped its edges round them, and at once they felt warm again. Though they had been surprised to find the carpet, they were more surprised still when they discovered all the pictures woven into it.

"They look like wonderful places," said little Fatima. She pointed to one of the pictures and said: "I should like to go there."

Well now, I told you it was a magic carpet, so you aren't surprised, are you, to learn that the instant Fatima said that it took right off? Yes, it did, with Fatima and Shamsuzzakir both still wrapped inside it.

And where did it go? Why, it went to the place that Fatima pointed to. And where was that? You just read on and you'll find out, because Fatima and Shamsuzzakir went to all the places in this book. All the stories are about what they saw, in every country in the world. In some of the stories, you'll meet Fatima and Shamsuzzakir again. Sometimes you won't see them, but they're always there, on their wonderful magic carpet.

ALGERIA

Tedjini Flamingo

Tedjini was born in a mud nest in a salt swamp in Algeria. When he looked out, he saw a big, strange creature. It had long, skinny legs, a long, skinny neck, and a big, heavy beak. It also had pink wings, and it was standing with its head held upside down in the water.

"Help!" cried Tedjini. "Go away, you ugly thing, or I'll call my mother!"

"She won't have far to come, then," said the strange creature. "*I'm* your mother!".

"But I'm little, and soft, and white. You're not like me at all!" said Tedjini.

"I looked like you when I was your age," she said. "Some day you'll look just like me."

"I don't want to change," said Tedjini.

So while the other baby flamingos learned to run and swim, Tedjini sat still. He thought that if he didn't move, he wouldn't change!

Now his mother was a wise old bird, so she kept on feeding him.

"He'll stir himself one day," she said.

And one day some hunters came to the swamp. Of course the birds saw them, and they all flew away. Even Tedjini ran on his great long legs, flapped his big pink wings, and soared away.

He flew and flew till the hunters were far behind. Then he landed on the water beside his mother. He said: "I'm glad I grew up after all, with long legs and big pink wings."

"Good," said his mother. "And you have a great big beak to stick upside down in the water. Now you can find your own food!"

Well, all the other flamingos had a honking good laugh at that. But Tedjini didn't mind at all. He was just very, very happy that he'd grown up to be a nice, ordinary flamingo.

The Salt and the Sea

Once there was an old fisherman called José who didn't like the sea.

You see, he had an old boat that was always turning upside down. And every time it did, José fell out. When he fell out, he landed in the sea. When he landed in the sea, he got his mouth full of water—nasty salty water, which he didn't like. Not one little bit.

In the end, he said he'd never go to sea again. Not while it was full of salt. So he just sat on the beach and glared at the sea.

Now José lived on the coast of Angola in West Africa, where the beach is very wide and flat. When the tide goes out it leaves puddles on the beach. The sun shines on them, dries up all the water, and leaves the salt behind.

One day, when José was walking on the beach, he came to one of the dried up puddles, and looked at the salt. "Bah!" he said, giving the salt a kick. "If you weren't in the sea, you salty old salt, I would go fishing again!"

Then he had a wonderful idea. He ran and found a bag. He scooped up all the salt from the dried puddle, and put it in the bag. Then he poured it in a pile, right at the back of the beach where the sea couldn't reach it.

He collected more salt, and more and more, till he had a great pile of it. Then sat on the pile and watched the tide come in.

"Yah, yah!" he shouted at the sea, "I've taken your salt! What are you going to do now?" The sea said nothing. Then the old man marched down to the sea, stuck in his finger, and sucked it. It still tasted salty!

Next day the old man once again took all the salt from the dried puddles and put it on his pile. But the sea still tasted salty. So he gathered salt the next day. And the next day.

The salt pile grew as big as a house, but still the sea stayed salty. At last the old man gave up. He sat down on his pile and wept, and even his tears were salty.

Then up came a fisherman. "Please," he said, "all the salt puddles have gone and my wife needs salt for cooking. Will you give me some in exchange for some fish?"

The old man was very hungry, after all his hard work, so he happily traded salt for fish. Soon everyone was trading with him because everyone uses salt for cooking.

So the old man never went fishing again, and he was happy for the rest of his days.

Should you go to Angola today, you wouldn't see the same old man, but you would see people working on the beach. And what are they doing? Why, collecting salt, of course!

ANTARCTICA

Kings and Penguins

Once upon a time—in fact it was a hundred million years ago—penguins could fly. They swam in the sea, too, and ran on the land.

At that time there were three kings—the King of the Air, the King of the Land, and the King of the Sea. One day they were talking about all the creatures they ruled.

"All the animals who walk on the land belong to me," said the King of the Land.

"That's right," said the King of the Air. "And all the birds who fly through the air are my subjects."

"Of course," agreed the King of the Sea. "But I claim all the creatures who swim in the sea. I'm sure you won't argue with that!"

The King of the Land and the King of the Air agreed, of course.

"Well then, the penguins belong to me!" cried the King of the Sea. "They spend more time in the sea than on land or in the air."

"Not at all!" cried the King of the Air. "They fly through the air. They're mine!"

"Nonsense! You're both wrong. Penguins run on the land—*my* land. They belong to me, and there's no point in arguing about it either," shouted the King of the Land.

"No, no, no, no, no!" cried the King of the Sea. "They're mine. I said so first."

And so, of course, he *had*.

But the King of the Air had quite lost his temper, so he bellowed: "All right. See if I care! But if I catch one of them flying through my air, you'll be in big trouble!"

"And," roared the King of the Land," I shan't let your penguins come on my land.

Well, that had the King of the Sea worried all right. But he wouldn't say so. He stormed off in a very bad temper, and went to talk to his penguins.

Now the penguins didn't mind at all that they couldn't fly in the air any more. They were quite happy to stay in the sea. "We'll catch more fish that way," they said. "But what shall we do if we can't walk on the land? We can't *always* stay in the water."

That's when the King of the Sea had his wonderful idea. "But you can walk *over* the land," he cried. "Come with me!"

So the penguins followed him, for many, many miles, to the cold, cold land of Antarctica, which is always covered with ice and snow. And as everyone knows, ice and snow are frozen water.

"There you are," said the King of the Sea. "You can live on the ice, which is mine. I do hope it's not too cold for you."

The penguins said it wasn't and they must have been right, for a hundred million years have passed, and Antarctica is still the home of the penguins.

The Beautiful Arctic Summer

A tiny round seed grew in a pod. When the pod burst open, the seed flew out. The wind picked her up, carried her away, and dropped her down again. She could feel soft, damp earth beneath her, and sat and waited for the sun to shine, so she could start growing. But instead, piles and piles of snow fell on her. It grew very, very cold. and very, very dark.

At last the sun shone, the snow melted, and the earth thawed. The little seed grew a root; she grew a stem, and a pair of leaves. Then she wasn't a seed any more. She was a plant. She looked round, but all she saw were rocks and one big plant. "Humf!" said the small plant. "This isn't a very nice place."

"Don't you know you're in the Arctic?" said the big plant.

"What does that mean?" said the little one, shivering slightly.

"It means you're near the top of the world. We have long cold winters, and in summer the sun shines all the time. But you'd better hurry, for summer's very short."

The small plant hurried up with her growing, and in a few weeks she was half the size of the big plant. She was just starting to grow her flower buds when the weather turned cold again.

"Brrr," she said, and the big plant said "You'll have to wait till next year!"

Well, the small plant didn't like that, but just then it started to snow. So she curled up tight, and the snow covered her over. She stayed like that till the snow melted and the sun shone again. She uncurled and looked round, but she could see only the rocks and the big plant. "What a horrible, ugly place," she said.

"No it's not," said the big plant. "Hurry up and grow some flowers, and you'll see."

So the little plant set to work and turned her buds into flowers. And when the flowers opened, guess what happened!

The flowers could look over the rocks. They could see for miles and miles. Everywhere they looked, the ground was covered with other flowers. Blue, yellow, pink, white and red flowers. And dancing everywhere, through the sunshiny air, were buzzy bees and butterflies.

"See?" said the big plant. "It's summer in the Arctic. What do you think of that?"

"It's just beautiful," sighed the happy little plant. And so it was.

The Whirly Blue Parasol

In Argentina, in South America, is a very large city called Buenos Aires. In Buenos Aires is a very large road, the Ninth of July Avenue. In fact, this Avenue is four hundred and sixty feet wide. Juan Luigi Henry MacDonald lives on one side of the Avenue. Every day he has to cross it to reach his school, which is on the other side.

It's very hot crossing that road, for the sun shines hot, bright and long on Buenos Aires. So Juan Luigi Henry MacDonald made himself a beautiful blue parasol. Whenever he crossed the Avenue to go to school, he carried his parasol to keep the sun from his head.

The parasol was very good at keeping the sun from Juan Luigi Henry MacDonald's head. But he was still hot, because even the air is hot in Buenos Aires, particularly the air over the Avenue.

So Juan Luigi Henry MacDonald invented himself a whirly parasol. He cut his blue parasol into long strips. Then he put wire round the edges of the strips.

Next time Juan Luigi Henry MacDonald crossed the Avenue, he held his whirly parasol over his head. He made the handle spin round in his hands. All the pretty blue strips twirled round, like helicopter blades, and made a little breeze. The parasol kept the sun from his head, and the breeze kept his head cool. Now Juan Luigi Henry MacDonald is the happiest boy in all of Buenos Aires.

Silly Billy Kangaroo

When Billy kangaroo was very small, he rode about in his mother's pouch. He drank up all his milk like a good little kangaroo, and he grew bigger. He grew so big, that he could eat grass instead of milk. But he still liked riding in his mother's pouch.

One day Mother kangaroo carried Billy all the way from their home to their eating place. Billy jumped down and ate himself full of grass. Then he wanted his mother to carry him home again.

"You're a big little kangaroo now," she

said, "You can hop home on your own."

"It's too far. I'll get tired," cried Billy, and sat down and sulked. He sat there for a long time waiting for her to change her mind and carry him home, but she said nothing. At last Billy turned to look at her. She wasn't there!

"Mother! Wait for me!" cried Billy, and he hopped along the path to home.

He didn't hear his mother come out from behind a bush, where she was hiding. He didn't hear her come hopping down the path behind him.

Billy saw a koala bear sitting in a gum tree. "Have you seen my mother?" Billy asked him. Of course the koala bear could see her, hopping along behind Billy. So he said: "Have you looked behind you?"

But Billy was sure his mother was somewhere ahead of him, so he said: "Of course she's not behind me! She wasn't behind me when I was there, so she can't be there now."

Well, the koala bear had to laugh at that, and Mother kangaroo smiled too. But Billy didn't look behind him. He hopped up the path, making a bollomp-bollomp sound.

A lyre bird heard him coming and heard another bollomp-bollomp behind Billy. So the lyre bird knew Billy's mother was there, even though he couldn't see her. She was round a corner of the path.

"Have you seen my mother?" Billy asked.

"No, I haven't seen her," said the lyre bird. "But I think she's behind you."

"She can't be behind me," said Billy. "I've just been there, and I didn't see her."

So he hopped off down the path again. When he was nearly home he saw a platypus swimming in the pond.

"Have you seen my mother?" asked Billy.

"Look behind you," said the platypus.

But Billy wouldn't look. He was *sure* his mother wasn't there!

"Then look in the water," said the platypus.

Billy looked down and there he saw himself, and, behind him, his mother.

"Oh," cried Billy, "you were behind me after all! Why didn't you say so?"

"I wanted to see if you could hop all the

way home on your own," said Mother kangaroo.

"Why, so I did," laughed Billy. And was very pleased with himself!

After that, Billy did all his own hopping. And he grew up to be one of the best hopping kangaroos in all Australia.

AUSTRIA

The Unhappy Chamois

In a wood—on a mountain—in the Alps—in the land of Austria—lived an unhappy, bad-tempered chamois. He was unhappy because his horns were straight. He was bad-tempered because he didn't have horns that curved at the tips, like all the other chamois have.

One fine day the chamois happened to walk under a walnut tree, just as the wind shook down a walnut. Donk! It hit him on the head, right between the horns.

"Ouch!" cried the unhappy chamois. "That hurt!" It also made him very angry. So he lowered his head, pawed the ground, and charged straight at the walnut tree!

Thump! He hit it a terrible blow. Down fell all the rest of the walnuts—bang, bang, rattle, rattle, donk—and hit him on the head.

"Ooo—ouch!" cried the chamois. "My poor head!" And he ran off to bathe his head in the lake, to make it feel better.

But when he reached the lake, he saw his reflection in the water, just like a mirror. And do you know—his horns weren't straight anymore! He'd bumped the tree so hard with them, they'd become curved at the tips!

BAHRAIN

Diving for Pearls

The country of Bahrain is really several islands, in the warm Persian Gulf. And in those warm waters are the oysters which make precious pearls. This is the story of a boy named Karim, who wanted to find lots of pearls, so his mother could have a pearl necklace, his sister a pearl bracelet, and his father a pearl ring.

Karim went to sea in a little rowing boat. He rowed for miles and miles, till he reached the place where the oysters grew. Then he dived to the bottom.

And do you know the first thing he saw? A mermaid waving to him! She had the end of her tail caught between some rocks! She was tugging and pulling, but she couldn't get it out.

Now Karim wasn't used to swimming under the sea, so he was almost out of breath. But he managed to swim to the mermaid. He

BELGIUM

The Tourist Carpet

When Fatima and Shamsuzzakir flew over Belgium on the magic carpet the first thing they saw was the huge port of Antwerp. There were hundreds of boats; docks and warehouses and railways; and everywhere were canals running off into the flat landscape.

"Let's see where that one goes," said Shamsuzzakir, and he gave the carpet a tug to make it turn and follow a big canal. They passed big factories and little farms, castles and villages, till they came to the great city of Brussels.

16

gave her tail a good strong tug.

The mermaid's tail came away from the rocks, and she was free. Before she swam away, she smiled at Karim, and put something into his hand. Karim was too out of breath to look at what it was. He swam back to the surface.

He climbed into his boat and looked in his hand. He was holding the end of a pearl necklace! The other end was still in the water. Karim pulled it and a great string of pearls came pouring into the boat. But the end was still in the water. He pulled and pulled and the necklace didn't end until the boat was full of beautiful, shining pearls.

Karim rowed home with his load of pearls. Now his mother has a pearl necklace. His sister has a pearl bracelet. His father has a pearl ring. And Karim has a beautiful suit of clothes, absolutely covered in pearls!

People from all over the world go to Brussels to see the beautiful old town hall but Shamsuzzakir and Fatima are the only ones who ever flew round it on a magic carpet! Fatima was just going to ask the carpet to land on the roof, so she could have a better look, when they heard a very strange sound, and looking round saw an even stranger thing—a big helicopter!

Of course neither Fatima nor Shamsuzzakir had ever seen a helicopter before— nor had the magic carpet! So off they flew to take a closer look. But just then a huge dark cloud appeared and they couldn't see the helicopter anymore; nor could they tell which direction it went.

"Maybe we'll see it again someday—in another country," said Fatima hopefully.

BOLIVIA

Mrs Quispe's Hat

Mrs Quispe lived on a farm high on a mountain near Lake Titicaca in Bolivia, which is in the middle of South America.

One day she filled a basket with fruit, put on her shawl and her black bowler hat, and set off to sell her fruit in the market.

But, when she was halfway there, Mrs Quispe sat down under a tree to rest. Her basket was heavy and she was tired. In fact, she was *so* tired, she dropped off to sleep.

Then along came a vicuna and lifted off her hat! "This looks good to eat," he said, and was about to take a big bite when he dropped the hat, and it fell down the side of the mountain. It didn't stop falling till it landed—splash!—right in Lake Titicaca.

But Mrs Quispe's hat wasn't the only thing floating on the lake. A poor mouse had also fallen in, and was swimming about, very tired, trying to get out again. So, when the hat fell right beside him, he wasted no time. "A boat has fallen out of the sky to rescue me!" he cried climbing into the hat. And there he sat, as happy as a mouse can be, till a wave came along and tipped him out.

But by that time the hat had sailed very close to land, so he swam ashore, and looked to see what his boat was doing.

It was gone! Mrs Quispe's hat had filled with water and sunk to the bottom.

Along came a fish and found Mrs Quispe's hat. "What a good place to hide this will make!" he said. So he swam underneath, and sat there laughing to himself, thinking how *Mr* Quispe, who was sitting on the shore with a fishing rod, couldn't catch him there!

Poor Mr Quispe hadn't caught a thing all day. But just then he felt something very heavy on his line and pulled it in. And what do you think it was? Mrs Quispe's hat!

"Fancy fishing out a hat!" he said. "I'll take it home for my wife. She likes hats!" He put it down beside him.

Then along came a lady eagle and spotted Mrs Quispe's hat. "Just the thing I need for my nest." she said. So she took it and flew to a tree high on the mountain. Then she went to find some grass to make a soft lining.

In the tree lived a snake. "What's that funny looking thing doing in my tree?" he said. And he pushed it out.

Now it so happens, that this was the very tree where Mrs Quispe had sat down to rest. There she still was, snoozing happily.

Down came her hat and landed—plonk!—right on her head, and woke her up. "Who did that?" she cried. "Who touched my hat?" But there was no one in sight. So she picked up her basket and went on her way. And Mrs Quispe never did know about her hat's strange adventures!

18

The Honey Bird

In Botswana, in the southern part of Africa, is the great Kalahari Desert. This is the home of the tiny, golden Bushmen, who are so clever they can talk with wild animals. This is the story of how a Bushman first made friends with a honey bird.

All honey birds adore honey, and one day one of them found a bees' nest running over with honey. He wanted some, but the bees chased him away.

It made the honey bird so angry, he sat on a branch and screamed with rage. "Those greedy bees have so much honey, they're letting it run away. I want some!"

"Is that so?" said a voice below. The honey bird looked down, and there was a little Bushman looking up. "Show me the nest, and I'll get honey for both of us."

Up soared the honey bird into the air, and led the Bushman to the bees' nest. The clever Bushman lit a fire, and the smoke put the bees to sleep. Then he took out some honey—some for the honey bird and some for himself.

The honey bird and the Bushman had a great feast, and then they both went back to their own people to tell them what had happened.

And from that day to this, the honey birds and the Bushmen have always been friends, and always share all the honey they find.

BRAZIL

The Naughty Steamboat

Brazil is an enormous country in South America. In Brazil is one of the biggest rivers in the world, the Amazon. All around it is thick jungle, which is very hard to move through. So instead of making roads to travel on, people make boats to sail on the Amazon.

One of the biggest boats on the Amazon was a beautiful steamboat called Vargas. She steamed up and down the river, carrying people and cattle and groceries and rubber. She was very busy, and very proud of herself. She liked to toot her whistle at all the other boats, to make them get out of the way quickly.

One day Vargas came hurrying and tooting up the river. She met a boy called Luis,

in his dugout canoe. The canoe's name was Lyra.

"Toot! Toot!" screamed Vargas. "Get out of my way. I'm in a hurry."

Luis paddled as hard as he could. But Vargas swept past, very close. She splashed water all over Luis and Lyra and almost tipped them over.

"Hoot! Hoot! Hoot!" laughed naughty Vargas. She thought it was very funny. She laughed so hard, she didn't look where she was going.

Suddenly—wallop! Vargas ran into a sand bank which was hidden just under the water. She stopped still.

Well, it was Luis' and Lyra's turn to laugh then! Luis laughed so hard, he nearly fell into the river. And Lyra herself laughed so hard, she nearly turned over!

Poor Vargas was really stuck. She struggled and churned, but she couldn't get off the sand bank. "Help! Help!" she cried.

Luis and Lyra stopped laughing. They went over to Vargas and tied a rope to her stern. Then Luis paddled as hard as he could, and Lyra pulled as hard as she could.

Suddenly, with a scrape, Vargas came off the sand bank. "Thank you very much," she said. "I'm sorry I splashed you."

Now Vargas, Luis and Lyra are very good friends, and Vargas never splashes them any more. And whenever she can she gives them a tow.

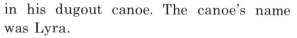

BULGARIA

The Curious Carpet

One day Fatima and Shamsuzzakir were cruising around on the magic carpet wondering which country they should visit next when Shamsuzzakir suddenly spotted the helicopter they had seen over Belgium. "Look," he cried, "Let's follow it."

They flew for a very long time, chasing along behind the helicopter and trying to catch up with it. But the helicopter was too fast for them. At last Fatima said: "I'm hungry."

"So am I. Let's land," said Shamsuzzakir. He tugged on the carpet to make it land, but the carpet wouldn't! It was curious about the strange, noisy flying creature!

It was night time when the helicopter swooped down and landed in a city. The carpet lost sight of it. "Well, perhaps you'll land now!" Fatima said to the carpet.

But the carpet still hadn't seen enough of the helicopter. It wanted to wait till morning. So it landed on the roof of a tall building, where it could have a good view.

Early next morning—buzz, buzz,—up zoomed the helicopter. Swish! Up darted the curious carpet, following it again. They went on and on, following the great blue Danube river between hills and mountains, through plains and towns. Fatima and Shamsuzzakir thought their journey would never end. But suddenly the helicopter landed in a field beside a beautiful town in Bulgaria.

Down came the curious carpet. It flew round the helicopter and had a good look. Then it made a sort of happy, sighing sound, and landed.

Not many people have seen a magic carpet, and certainly nobody from that town had ever seen one. They all stood round and goggled at the carpet, and at the strangely dressed boy and girl who were sitting on it.

At last a woman spoke to them. "Welcome to Bulgaria," she said. "I am Mrs Popov. Would you like to come to my house for dinner?"

"Oh, yes please," said Fatima and Shamsuzzakir together. "We're very, very hungry."

They rolled up their carpet—it was quite tired—and carried it to Mrs Popov's house.

Fatima and Shamsuzzakir were tired, too, and hungry, and rather dusty. So Mrs Popov gave them a lovely hot bath. Then she gave them dinner, and put them both to bed.

The carpet didn't get anything to eat—for whoever heard of feeding a carpet? But Mrs Popov gave it a tidy-up with her vacuum cleaner, and the carpet loved it!

The Magic Fish

Ne Nu was a poor Burmese fisherman. He worked hard, catching lots of fish. Some he took home for his family to eat. Some he took to the market to trade for rice—also for them to eat.

Ne Nu had a great many children. All of them were growing bigger and eating more every day. Poor Ne Nu had to work harder and harder to keep them fed.

"Perhaps if I fish by night as well as by day, I will catch enough fish for my hungry family," said Ne Nu. So, one moonlit night, he went out in his boat and flung his net in the water. At once he felt something heavy in his net. He pulled it in, and there was a big, beautiful fish. It was a very heavy, but very strange fish. For it was not a fish to be eaten. No—it was a stone fish, made of lovely, pale green jade.

Ne Nu had never seen anything so wonderful in his life. He ran home to show it to his family.

But the children didn't like his beautiful jade fish. "What good is a stone fish?" they said. "We can't eat that."

"Jade is very precious," said his wife. "Take it to the market and sell it. Then you can buy lots of rice for the children."

So Ne Nu put the jade fish in a basket and set off through the jungle for the market. On the way, the fish spoke to him. "I am a magic fish," it said, "and although I am made of stone, I swim in the river. If you put me back your children will never be hungry again."

Ne Nu dipped the basket in the river, and the jade fish swam away. When he lifted the basket from the water, it was full of rice! He rushed home to tell his wife what had happened, and when she emptied the basket, it filled up again with rice. It was a magic, never-emptying basket!

Then Ne Nu and his wife and all his children had all the food they ever wanted, so they lived happily ever after.

The Disappearing Peanuts

Mary lived in Burundi, which is a small country in the middle of Africa. One day she didn't want to eat her dinner. She wanted peanuts instead. "You eat your dinner," said her mother, "and then you may have some peanuts."

Mary did as she was told. But when she had finished her dinner, she was so full, she couldn't eat the peanuts! So she put them in her pocket. Later she was hungry, and looked for the peanuts. But her pocket was empty.

Mary and her mother looked everywhere for the peanuts, but they couldn't find them.

Then one day Mary's mother called from the garden: "I've found your peanuts!" Mary looked. There, growing by the sweet potatoes, were some new peanut plants!

"They must have fallen out of your pocket here," said her mother. "Now they're growing!"

Mary looked after the peanut plants. She watered and weeded them, and watched them grow. When they were ready, she pulled them up. And there, on the roots, were lots and lots and lots of peanuts for Mary to eat!

Proud Weaver Bird

Once upon a time a very proud baya weaver bird built a fine nest in a tree in Cambodia. He wanted his nest to be best of all the nests in the tree. So when he wove the rope to hang it from, he built it longer than any other. When he made his round nest at the end of the rope, he made it bigger than any other.

The other birds finished their nests first. They sat in the tree and called: "Hurry-up-up-up! Our wives are coming-ing-ing!"

"I'm almost done-done-done!" he chattered. He had only his entrance tube to build. He hurried as fast as he could. He'd just woven the last straw into place when the baya weaver wives arrived.

"Are our nests ready-eady-eady?" they sang. "We want to lay our eggs-eggs-eggs!"

The proud baya weaver felt specially proud when his wife saw his big nest.

"Lovely-ly-ly," she twittered, and popped into the tube to climb up to the nest.

"Squawk-awk-awk! Help-elp-elp!" came her muffled cry. She was stuck in the tube! In his great hurry, he'd made it too small!

Then what a commotion! All the birds flew round the nest to help her. They pulled away lumps of straw until she was free.

She sat on a branch to smooth her ruffled feathers and scold her husband. And he, poor fellow, was busy rebuilding his beautiful nest.

CAMEROUN

The Pygmies and the Okoumé Tree

In the deep, dark forests of Cameroun live a tribe of tiny Pygmy people. One day, after a rainstorm, they heard a great voice. "Ooo, ouch!" it cried. "Please come and help me!"

The Pygmies were frightened, so they ran and hid. But one brave little man crept out and looked, and found where the voice came from. You'd never guess who it was crying, so I'll tell you. It was a giant okoumé tree!

The brave Pygmy was surprised. "I've never heard a tree talk before," he said.

"We trees usually keep quiet about it," the okoumé tree replied. "But the rain has washed a huge rock down the hill, and it's squashing my roots. Will you move it for me?"

The tiny Pygmy felt sorry for the great tree, so he went and brought back all the other Pygmies. They all pushed and pushed and *pushed* on the rock, till at last it rolled away.

"Ah! What a relief! Thank you," said the okoumé tree. "I feel much better now."

From that time to this very day, the giant tree and the tiny Pygmies have been friends. And whenever the Pygmies want to know what's happening a long way away, they ask the okoumé tree. He's such a giant, he can see far over and into the forest, and he always tells them what's happening there.

24

The Porcupine and the Skunk

One summer silly Bob went looking for gold in the north of Canada. He was silly because he went alone, into a forest he didn't know.

It's not surprising that, before very long, he was lost. He wandered through the forest, calling for help. No one answered. At last he sat on a rock, feeling very sorry for himself. "I'll never get out of here," he moaned.

"Neither will I if you don't help me," said a voice. It was right under his feet!

Bob looked down. There was a deep hole in the rocks. At the bottom was an untidy, spiky-looking animal. "Poor fellow, you've fallen in and can't get out," said Bob. He reached down to pull out the animal.

"Don't touch me!" it shouted. "Put down a branch for me." Bob put an old branch down the hole. Then he pulled it out, with the animal holding on to the end by its teeth.

"Thank you," it said, spitting out bits of bark. "I'm a porcupine. You mustn't touch me, because I'm covered in quills, like little arrows. You don't want them stuck in your hand."

"I sure don't," said Bob. The porcupine's quills looked quite dangerous to him.

Then he said: "I'm lost. Can you help me?"

"I'll lead you to the edge of the forest," said the porcupine. "But could you do just one more thing for me, before we go?"

"What's that?" asked Bob.

"Pull my friend out of the hole," said the porcupine. "We fell in together!"

Bob looked down the hole. There was a little black and white animal looking back at him! He plunged his arm into the hole to grab it.

"Careful!" screeched the porcupine. "Handle him gently, or you'll be sorry!"

Bob lifted out the little animal carefully. It looked very pretty and friendly. He couldn't see what was dangerous about it. Silly Bob—he didn't know a skunk when he saw one! He should have known better.

Suddenly, a great big hungry bear rushed out of the trees, snarling at them.

"Run!" screamed the porcupine.

Bob ran, but the others didn't. The porcupine swatted the bear on the nose with his tail. His quills stuck in the bear's nose!

"Yow-ow-ow!" cried the bear. He stopped.

The skunk lifted his tail and squirted the bear with a horrible, *horrible* smell. The bear turned and ran away.

"Phwew!" gasped Bob. He ran from the smell too. The porcupine and the skunk ran with him, laughing their heads off.

"We know how to look after ourselves, even though we are small!" giggled the skunk.

Then they led Bob to the edge of the forest and said goodbye, but Bob never forgot his clever little friends.

CENTRAL AFRICAN REPUBLIC

The Shrikes and the Snake

In the middle of Africa is a wide savanna land of trees and giant grass. A long time ago a boy named Riri lived there with his family. They all worked in the fields—even Riri, who was the watchboy. He kept the birds from eating the sorghum seeds.

Every morning he picked up his stick and went to the fields. As soon as the sun came up, along came the birds. They swooped down on the fields and started eating the sorghum seeds. Riri dashed at them, waving his stick, and frightened the birds away.

One day, most of the birds flew away when they saw Riri's big stick. But the shrike birds wouldn't go away. They just hopped and fluttered out of Riri's way, and then started eating the seeds again!

There they sat, twenty fat black and white shrikes, eating as hard and as fast as they could. Riri didn't like them at all, for they had strange yellow rings round their staring black eyes. He didn't like the way they snapped their black beaks at him. He didn't like the way they chattered at him. *And he didn't like the way they ate the seeds!* He threw his stick at them!

Up flew the shrikes, squawking and snapping. "Aha," laughed Riri. "Now they'll go away!"

But they didn't. They flew at Riri, snapping and pecking at him. They frightened him so, he ran away and hid in the long grass under a tree. He sat there and he cried and cried. He was afraid to go home and tell his family he couldn't keep the horrid birds away.

Then right over his head he heard a slithery voice. "Do you need help?" it said.

Riri jumped up, The voice belonged to a great black and gold and green snake. It was wrapped all round a branch. "Don't be frightened," it said. "If you help me, I promise to help you." The snake told him how it had tied itself to a branch so it wouldn't fall from the tree as it slept. But when it woke up, it couldn't untie itself. The knots were too tight!

"So if you will untie me," said the snake, "I will scare off all those rascally shrikes who are gobbling up your sorghum seeds."

Riri was afraid of the snake, but he was a brave boy. So he climbed up the tree and untied it. At once it slid down, without a word of thanks, and disappeared in the grass. Riri thought it had lied to him, and run away. But suddenly all the shrikes shrieked and flew from the field. The snake was chasing them! Then it slithered away.

Do you know, Riri never saw the snake again. But it must still be lurking somewhere near. For to this day, the shrikes in that part of the world stay up in the trees—and they don't eat sorghum seeds any more!

CEYLON

The Fishermen's Tea Party

Two fat merchants met on a narrow bridge above the Mahaweli Ganga river. Each one carried a great pack on his back. They were cross because it was the middle of the monsoon season, and the rain was pouring down. There wasn't room on the bridge to let them pass.

One of them had a pack full of tea. It was all wrapped up in a rubber sheet, because he didn't want it to get wet. The other one had a pack full of tin teapots. He wasn't bothered about his pots getting wet. But he didn't like *himself* getting wet.

"Out of my way," roared the tin teapot merchant.

"Who do you think you're talking to, you great buffoon?" screeched the tea merchant.

They both got very angry, and neither would back off the bridge. They pushed each other, grunting, and panting, and pushing and shoving. The poor bridge creaked and groaned, and finally fell apart.

Splash! Everything fell in the water— bridge, tea, pots, merchants and all!

The merchants staggered out of the river and started to fight. They forgot all about their tea and tin teapots.

Later that day, two sad fishermen sat in their boat in Trincomalee harbour, where the Mahaweli Ganga runs into the sea. They were sad because they were wet, and because they hadn't caught many fish.

"I could just do with a nice hot cup of tea right now," said the first fisherman.

"So could I," said the second fisherman.

Just then up floated two packs. The fishermen caught them and opened them. What do you think they found? A bale of tea and two dozen tin teapots, of course! The happy fishermen rushed home and made themselves pots and pots of tea. Then they had a tea party and drank it all.

And the two merchants are still fighting.

Desert Flower's Gold Ring

In the north of Africa, in the land of Chad, lived a beautiful girl named Desert Flower. She had big, dark eyes and soft, dark skin. Her thick, black hair was twisted, right from the top to the bottom, in hundreds of tiny plaits. But although she was the most beautiful girl in Chad, she was the saddest one, too.

You see, every girl in that part of Chad wore a small gold ring on the side of her nose. But Desert Flower's ring was a *big* gold ring.

"Our daughter is the most beautiful girl, so she must have the most beautiful ring," said Desert Flower's mother and father.

Desert Flower was sad because she didn't like wearing such a big ring. When she walked, it swung and bumped and tickled her nose.

One day, when she went to the well for water, the ring swung and bumped and tickled her more than ever. It made her sneeze. She sneezed so hard, the ring jumped from her nose and fell down the well!

She ran home and told her father. He lowered a bucket into the well, and tried to scoop out the ring. But he couldn't reach it.

Now Desert Flower has no ring at all in her nose. It makes her parents very sad, but Desert Flower is happy, because her nose doesn't tickle her any more. Now she's not only the most beautiful girl in Chad, but the *happiest* also.

CHILE

Pedro's Wonderful Land

This is the story of Fatima and Shamsuzzakir's visit to Chile—a long, narrow country on the coast of South America. The magic carpet took them, one day, high above the great Andes Mountains to the northern part of Chile. There, among the snowy peaks, was a lake. Beside it was a shepherd boy. He told them that the lake was called Sajama. His name was Pedro.

"Is all of Chile like this—all lakes and mountains?" asked Shamsuzzakir.

"Oh no," said Pedro. "Chile has mountains down one side, and sea down the other side. But in between are many different and wonderful places, for it's many, many miles long!"

Fatima and Shamsuzzakir asked Pedro to show them all those wonderful places. So he hopped on the carpet and away they flew. First they went to the huge copper mine called Chuquicamata. It looked like a great bowl cut out of the rocks, with its sides cut in great steps—like a stairway for a giant.

Then they flew south, over great deserts where no rain falls, till they came to the part called the campo chileno. There they saw the fine cities of Santiago and Valparaiso; rich farmlands and prairies; and many canals carrying water from the melted snow of the mountains to the fields. They landed beside a lovely white farmhouse. The farmer invited them on to his veranda, which was covered in vines and flowers. And there they had lunch—tomatoes and maize and three kinds of melons!

When they left the farmer, they went on south, over wide prairies and farms, and great areas of thick jungle, all dark and wet.

At last, Pedro said they were coming to the end of his country, which is also the southernmost tip of South America. They saw that the mountains were not so high as before. And where the land met the sea, it broke up into hundreds and hundreds of islands, big and small.

Pedro guided the carpet to the farthest island, and there it came to rest. Then Fatima and Shamsuzzakir saw what a strange and lonely place it was. Pedro told them it was Cape Horn. "This is where the ships come when they want to pass around the end of South America," he told them.

Fatima and Shamsuzzakir looked at the cold grey sea, and the great cold waves, and shivered in the cold, cold wind. They were glad they had a magic carpet and didn't have to travel round Cape Horn by ship.

CHINA

The Boy and the Dragon

Once, in ancient days, a terrible dragon came down from the mountains and attacked a city in China.

Nobody had ever seen a more frightening, terrible dragon. He was covered in glittering scales of many colours. He had great, glaring eyes, and lots of powerful legs with dozens and dozens of long, sharp claws. His huge mouth was full of pointed teeth. His long red tongue had two points at the end. And as if that wasn't enough he snorted fire from his nose.

All the people ran inside the city walls and slammed shut the great gates. "Grrr!

Now I must burn down the gates before I can eat all you tasty people," bellowed the dragon.

The people stood on top of the city walls, where the dragon couldn't reach them. They cried: "Wait, wait! Don't eat us! There's a little fat boy hiding behind a rock over there. Why don't you eat him?"

The dragon looked behind the rock and there was the little fat boy. He was hiding there because the gates had shut before he could enter the city. You see, he was such a fat little boy, he couldn't run fast.

"Yum, yum" chortled the dragon. He opened his enormous mouth to eat the boy.

"Wait, wait!" cried the fat boy. "You mustn't eat me. I'm a *magic* boy!"

The dragon stopped. He wondered if a magic boy would upset his digestion. And

COLOMBIA

The Oil Well Who Wasn't

This is the story of an oil well who wasn't. Well, he was a well all right, but he wasn't an oil well. He wasn't anything at all until some men came into the Colombian forest with lots of machines, and drilled a hole in the ground. They were looking for oil. They drilled down and down, for hundreds of feet. Suddenly a great column of liquid shot out of the hole and made a beautiful fountain over their heads. "Whoopee! We've hit a gusher!" cried the men.

Then they all stopped cheering and became very gloomy. They picked up their drill and drove away, leaving the gushing well. You see, it wasn't an oil well, it was a water well.

The poor well felt so lonely, he stopped gushing. "Why bother?" he muttered. Nobody wants me." He cried and dribbled.

"Oh, don't do that! We liked you very much," cried all the birds in the trees.

"Swish!" said the well, "someone wants me after all!" He gushed up more than ever, and fountained and sparkled in the sun. And the birds sang for joy.

30

anyway, he loved magic tricks. Then the boy told him that he was ten thousand years old, and he could do all kinds of magic. "I was just coming to Chungking to be a magician for the people here." he said. "But since they told you to eat me, I don't like them any more."

"I don't blame you," said the dragon. "Do some magic for me, and I won't eat you."

"All right," said the magic boy. He threw a handful of red powder into the air and—snap! Out of the dragon's back popped two great wings. Then the boy climbed on the dragon's back and they flew away.

When the people of Chungking saw that, they cried to the boy to come back. They wanted him to do magic for them. But the boy and the dragon disappeared over the mountains, and were never seen again.

CONGO

Nosy Mordecai

In the hot Congo lived a baby elephant named Mordecai. He was very nosy. When he saw a new thing, he just had to know what it was. One day in the jungle, he saw something shiny in a bush. His mother was eating leaves, and didn't see him slip away to investigate.

Mordecai thought the shiny thing might go away if it saw him. So he tiptoed round some bushes until he reached it. It was a long, round metal tube. One end was hidden in the bushes, so he pulled the other end with his trunk.

The shiny thing swung up in the air and made a really terrible bang! Then a frightened man jumped out of the bushes and ran away.

Up thundered Mordecai's mother. "That was a hunter!" she trumpeted. "You took his gun and frightened him!" And she trampled off to tell everyone what a brave hero Mordecai was.

Mordecai was very proud to be a hero. But he was still as nosy as ever.

The Kitten-Beast

Inez lived in Costa Rica, which is in Central America. One day as she was going home from school through the forest she heard a crying sound in the bushes. When she looked she found a kitten—but the strangest kitten she'd ever seen. He was brown, with lines of black spots, and had rings on his little tail.

When Inez went to pick him up, the kitten tried to scratch her. But she didn't want to leave him, for he looked unhappy and hungry. So she took her books from her satchel and scooped him up in it. She ran

all the way home and into the kitchen. "Look what I found!" she cried to her mother, and opened the bag. The kitten leaped out on to the table.

"A wild beast!" screamed her mother. She grabbed Inez, pulled her outside, and slammed the door. "I'm not going in there again until father comes home," she said. When he came she told him about the beast.

He opened the kitchen door very carefully, and peeped in. Then he burst out laughing and called them into the kitchen. The kitten lay fast asleep on the table, with milk all over his face. He had knocked over a jug of milk and drunk as much as he wanted.

"He's a puma kitten," said her father, "and only about two weeks old. I wonder how he got here. And where his mother is?"

Well, they asked all the villagers, and all the local farmers. But no one had seen a mother puma. So it was a great mystery how the kitten came to be there.

Inez wanted to keep him for a pet, but her father said he would be nine feet long by the time he was two years old. "Pumas can never be tamed," he said. But he let her keep him for a while. Inez called him Josef, and she fed him and took care of him.

By the time he was eight months old, Josef had lost his baby spots and was a golden brown colour all over. He was very heavy, and very long. It was time to set him free. So Inez and her father took him in their car, and drove many miles into the forest.

They let him out. Josef stood looking at them for a moment. Then he sniffed the air, and bounded off into the forest. "Won't he be hungry?" Inez asked.

"We'll feed him, until he learns to hunt for himself," said her father.

So they left some food for Josef, and went away. Every week they brought more food, and left it in the same place. They could tell that Josef came to eat it, for they saw the marks of his paws. One day, they found he hadn't touched the food they'd left the week before. Then they knew he could look after himself, and didn't need help any more and was living free and happy.

Sugar Cane

Cuba is a big island in the Caribbean Sea. Lots of sugar cane for making sugar grows there. Maria lived on a sugar plantation, and there was hardly anything in the world she liked better than sugar cane. One day she slipped into the cane fields, broke a stem from a juicy plant, and chewed and sucked all the sweet syrup from it.

Her mother was very angry when Maria came home. For she was simply *covered* with sticky syrup. It was all over her face, all over her hands, all over her dress and all over her shoes. It was even in her ears!

Maria's mother scolded her. She shoved Maria into the bath and scrubbed her all over. She told her not to do it again.

Next day, Maria's mother told her to stay in the house, "Someone special is visiting us today," she said. Maria waited and waited, but no one came. At last she grew tired of sitting around, so she slipped out of the house.

"I'll just have one little piece of sugar cane," she thought, "and then I'll go back." But after she had one piece, she thought two pieces also seemed a good idea. So she had another piece, and another and another. She chewed and sucked sugar cane until she was full.

She went home, all coated with syrup. But her mother didn't scold. She just said: "Our special visitor was your big cousin Julio. We went to Havana, and we saw all the sights, and we had some chocolate ice cream."

Maria burst into tears. There were two things she loved more than sugar cane. One was her big cousin Julio. The other was ice cream. She was so unhappy, she didn't even squirm when her mother bathed her and scrubbed her ears. And she never ate sugar cane again.

Then one day cousin Julio came back again. "I hear you've been a very good girl," he said. So he took her to Havana and gave her lots of chocolate ice cream.

The Tree of Good Wishes

At the eastern end of the Mediterranean Sea is the large island of Cyprus. This beautiful island has a long history. A thousand years before Christ, the ancient Greek and Phoenician sailors came to the island, and found men living there.

But even before that, before the first men and women stood on Cyprus, an ancient tree grew there. It grows there still, thousands and thousands of years later. It will live forever.

The ancient tree is a magic tree. It looks like a very ordinary tree—old and gnarled and bent—but yet an ordinary tree. Only once, every hundred years, does it look different. Then it has a single fruit, which looks like a big, bright purple pear. This wonderful fruit remains on the tree just one day, before it withers and drops.

The lucky man or woman or child who discovers that fruit, one day in one hundred years, is very lucky indeed. For this is the tree of all good wishes.

The one who eats the magic fruit has his every good wish come true, for all his life. But if he ever wishes a bad wish, he loses all his luck, and is miserable for all his life.

The tree of good wishes is somewhere in Cyprus. Would you dare to eat its fruit?

CZECHOSLOVAKIA

The Golden Bone

Over Czechoslovakia flew the wonderful magic carpet, taking Fatima and Shamsuzzakir on a new adventure. Suddenly it swooped, and landed by a road. Along the road came a big, thin dog. He looked very weak and hungry.

Fatima felt sorry for him. She called out: "Hello, dog. Do you like sandwiches?"

"I surely do," said the dog, pricking up his ears and looking hopeful.

"Then come and share our lunch," she said, opening the lunch basket.

The hungry dog ate several sandwiches, and a whole packet of biscuits. "Ah, that's better," he sighed. Then he asked: "Could you take me to Prague?"

Of course they could! It was no trouble at all for the magic carpet. In a moment, they were on the way. The dog stretched himself happily on the soft carpet. "This is a lot better than walking," he said. "By the way, would you like to know why I'm going to Prague?"

Of course they wanted to know! So the dog told them this strange story:

"You know, don't you, that Prague is a very old city?" he asked. "Well, one of my family lived there, hundreds of years ago. He belonged to a prince, and one day he saved the prince's life. So the prince had a beautiful bone made, of pure gold, and gave it to my ancestor. And do you know what my ancestor did with the bone? He buried it! Now I'm going to look for it. You see, everyone in my village is very hungry this year because the crops have failed. If I find the bone, I shall sell it to buy food for them."

"You're a very kind dog," said Shamsuzzakir admiringly. "But why did your ancestor leave the bone? Why wasn't it dug up long ago?"

"Because," said the sensible dog, "we didn't need it. Until now."

Just then they arrived over Prague. Fatima and Shamsuzzakir wondered how they could find the bone in such a huge city. But the dog wasn't worried. Down through the centuries, the story of the bone and its exact hiding place had passed from dog to dog. Now he directed the carpet straight to an ancient palace.

"That's it, I'm sure!" he cried. "Land in the garden!" Down they went. The dog hopped from the carpet and ran to a crumbling old statue. "The bone should be right here," he said, digging behind the statue.

And, would you believe it, there was the bone, as good as new! They rubbed the earth from it, and the gold shone and sparkled.

They took the bone back to the dog's home, and used it to buy food. There was enough to feed the whole village for a year!

Then Fatima and Shamsuzzakir flew on their way, but they never forgot the kind dog and his ancestor's wonderful bone.

Bush Baby

In Dahomey, in Africa, live bush babies—tiny, cuddly animals with soft fur and huge eyes. They can jump very high.

Henri bush baby was sitting in his tree one day. Suddenly, *crash ! ! !* A heavy branch fell from the top of the tree and landed beside him. It gave Henri such a fright, he jumped straight up in the air. Up and up he went, until he could see all Dahomey spread out below him! Up and up he went, until he could see all *Africa* below him ! ! Up and up he went until he could see the *whole round earth* below him ! ! !

Henri landed with a bump on a cloud! He held on tight, for he was afraid of falling all the way back to earth.

"I'll take you down," said a soft, fluffy voice. It was the cloud talking to him!

"Thank you very much," said Henri. "I'll show you the way."

They were almost down again when the cloud began to rain. It shrank and shrank, until there was only a tiny piece left, carrying Henri. "Sorry about this," it whispered, "but I can't help raining when I'm so near the ground."

They reached Henri's tree and he hopped on to it. Then, with a last shower of raindrops, the rest of the cloud disappeared.

Henri sat in his tree and wept great tears. The cloud had saved him, but it couldn't save itself. His friends came to see why Henri cried, and he told them of the brave cloud.

So all the bush babies sat and wept, till their tears made a puddle. But the sun shone on the puddle and dried it up, and made a little cloud! It floated up to the bush babies.

"Thank you for your tears," it whispered in its soft, fluffy voice. "They have made me whole again." And it drifted off into the sky.

Nathalie's Bicycle Ride

Denmark is a very flat country in the north of Europe. It has one great city, called Copenhagen, which is built right beside the sea. Because it's so flat, Copenhagen is a good place for bicycle riding. Nearly everyone there has a bicycle.

Arne lived in Copenhagen. On Saturdays and Sundays, he went riding on his super racing bicycle. It had low, hooked handle-bars and a light frame. With big Arne pumping away at the pedals, that bicycle could go like a rocket! He was so proud of it, he wouldn't use it during the week. It might get scratched!

Arne had a little sister, named Nathalie. Every day she said to Arne: "Let me have a ride on your lovely bicycle."

Arne always replied: "No, you're too small. You would fall off and hurt yourself." And he would lock it away in the shed.

But, once, he left the shed unlocked. Nathalie soon discovered the open door. She wheeled the bicycle into the garden. "I'm sure I won't fall off," she said. "I'll just have a little ride round the garden." And then she added: "Anyway, if I do fall off, I'll just fall among the flowers, and that won't hurt!"

(But it's a good thing her mother didn't hear Nathalie say that! She was very proud of her beautiful flower garden.)

The bicycle heard Nathalie, though!

"Aha!" thought the bicycle. "Naughty Nathalie needs to be taught a lesson!"

Nathalie climbed on the bicycle and rode it round the garden. "Whee!" she laughed. "This is easy!" Of course it was easy. The bicycle was doing all the work.

When she tried to stop the bicycle, it didn't stop. It turned out of the garden and into the road, and ran away with her.

Nathalie was so surprised, she would have fallen off if she could. But she was stuck tight to the saddle.

The runaway bicycle rolled down the road, going faster and faster. It went straight for a deep canal. Nathalie screamed. She tried to take her feet from the pedals. But her feet kept turning, faster and faster. And the canal came closer and closer.

Right at the edge of the canal, the bicycle stopped dead, and Nathalie came unstuck. She soared over the handlebars, did six somersaults and landed in the canal!

Poor, silly, naughty Nathalie. She swam back across the canal and climbed out, all soaked and muddy. She took hold of the bicycle, and pushed it home. Then she cleaned it, polished it, put it away, and never touched it again.

The Clever Pelican

The Vain Flycatcher

A pelican named Senor Alcatraz lived in a mangrove swamp where the shores of Dominica meet the Caribbean Sea. He and Senora Alcatraz had a nest there, full of hungry baby pelicans. Senor and Senora Alcatraz caught fish from the sea, and brought them back to the nest in the big pouches in their throats. Then they opened their beaks and the little pelicans reached in, took the fish, and ate them.

One day, flying over the sea, Senor Alcatraz saw a fine, big fish. He dived for it. Wallop! He landed with a tremendous splash and caught it. Then he sat on the sea with his mouth open while the water drained away—being very careful not to drop the fish. Not careful enough, though, for along flew a greedy seagull and stole it!

Nest day, Senor Alcatraz saw the gull following him again. "I'll fix him!" he thought. He dived down and caught a piece of driftwood, pretending it was a fish. Sure enough, down zoomed the gull and tried to steal it. Thud! He hit the wood very hard.

"Ouch! That hurt," screeched the gull as he flew away. And he never again tried to steal from clever Senor Alcatraz.

A beautiful paradise flycatcher lived on the island of Sumatra, in the East Indies. Part of the day he flew about the forest to catch insects. The rest of the time he flew around just to show off. He was bright red all over, except for his head, which was black. His tail feathers were very, very long and lovely. My, he *was* vain and proud of himself.

One day a little bird brought some news to the forest. "The island chief has just built a beautiful house!" he chattered. "It's the most beautiful thing I ever saw!"

"You little fool!" cried the flycatcher, in a great rage. "You said it was the most beautiful thing you ever saw! What about me? Is it more beautiful than I am?"

The little bird was frightened, for the flycatcher was twice his size. But he didn't like being called a fool. So he said: "It's *twice* as beautiful as you, you silly old thing!" Then he shot into a tiny hole in a tree, where the flycatcher couldn't reach him.

"You horrible little bird!" screamed the flycatcher. "I hope you get stuck in there forever!"

Well, really! Wasn't that a terrible thing

to say? What a big bully!

"You great vain bully, you!" cried all the other birds. They flew at the flycatcher. They chased him all over the forest, and round and round the chief's new house (which was, indeed, very beautiful). "Wait till we catch you," they cried. "We'll pull out your fine tail feathers!"

They frightened the flycatcher so much, he turned pure white. Yes he did. Pure white with black trimmings.

Now that made the birds feel very ashamed of themselves. The flycatcher was ashamed too, because he *had* been vain, and a bully. So he blushed. He blushed so hard, he turned red all over again!

Then he flew back to the hole in the tree and apologized to the little bird. Soon they were friends, and all was well.

Now the paradise flycatcher is as beautiful as ever, but he's not so vain about it. And just to remind him, his red feathers turn white again, all over, once every year.

Blowpipes and Bubbles

The Jivaro Indians live hidden deep in the far forests of Ecuador in South America. They live by hunting with long blowpipes and sharp darts. One day a young trader named Patricio set out to find them. His friends begged him not to go. "The Jivaros will shoot you with their darts," they said.

But Patricio laughed. "They won't shoot when they see what I have to trade with them," he said. And away he went, carrying a pack on his back.

At last Patricio came to their village of the Jivaro Indians.

It seemed empty, but he knew eyes watched him from every house. He sat on the ground and took a bottle of liquid soap from his pack. He squeezed some into a bowl. Then he dipped a clay pipe into it and blew a bubble!

In a moment all the Indians rushed out of hiding to watch the beautiful rainbow bubble. It grew bigger and bigger, till it was as big as Patricio's head. Then it went pop! The Indians sighed with disappointment. But Patricio blew another bubble, and sent it floating in the air.

What fun! Soon all the Indians were blowing bubbles with their blowpipes. Patricio became their friend. And he traded all his bottles of soap for beautiful baskets made by the Indians, and took them home.

The Sphinx

On their adventurous travels round the world, Fatima and Shamsuzzakir arrived over Egypt on their magic carpet. From the air Egypt looked a strange, striped country. The centre stripe was the broad, blue Nile. On each side of that were crammed houses and fields and orchards, in bright green stripes. Then, on the outside, were very wide brown stripes, stretching farther than they could see. This was the desert.

"Now let's go and see the mysterious sphinx," said Fatima. "People say it has a secret to tell, but no one has ever heard it speak."

The sphinx is an ancient, huge statue, worn and crumbling, that sits in the desert. They soon found it, and what a marvel it was, with a man's head and a lion's body!

They zoomed round and round its head. "It does look as if it might speak," Shamsuzzakir said. "I wonder what it would say?"

Then, with an ancient creak and rumble, the sphinx moved its head! It raised a great paw and swatted at the magic carpet!

"Go away, insect. Stop buzzing in my ear!" it growled in a shiver-making voice!

The magic carpet shot out of reach, with Fatima and Shamsuzzakir clinging together in fright and surprise. They flew away fast and never went near the sphinx again!

The Strawberry Baron

Many hundreds of years ago, England was divided into many little domains. One of them was ruled by terrible Baron de Bludge.

Baron de Bludge liked nobody. He liked nothing—except strawberry jam. All day long he ate it, potful after potful.

The only time he stopped eating was when he left his fortress to see how his strawberries were growing. For miles around, no farmer was allowed to grow anything except strawberries. Woe betide any poor man who the baron caught growing grain or beans!

Baron de Bludge toured his domain on his big white horses. And when I say *horses,* I mean *four* white horses. He was too big and fat for one horse. So a special seat was made to be carried on the backs of four white horses, and Baron de Bludge rode on that. What a strange and terrifying sight he was to his strawberry-growing subjects!

They worked very hard, and grew tons and tons of strawberries. By the cartload they went to the fortress. By the cartload they were made into jam to fill the baron's pantry.

One winter, all the farmers were starving. They never had much to eat at any time, but that winter they had nothing at all.

They went to the fortress and called to Baron de Bludge: "Give us some strawberry jam!"

"No, you cheeky farmers!" roared Baron de Bludge, putting down his spoon and his pot of jam. He ran to his door to chase them away. Bung! Baron de Bludge had grown so fat, he stuck in the door! "Gerrrroww!" he roared, flexing his great muscles. But he couldn't move an inch forward—and he couldn't move *half* an inch back. He was well and truly stuck!

When the farmers saw that, how they laughed. They jeered and made faces at bad Baron de Bludge. Then they went into the fortress—through the back door—and took all the jam.

When big, bad, terrifying Baron de Bludge saw that, he broke down and cried. He begged: "Don't take all my jam. Please."

In all his life, he had never before said please. And it worked, first time! The kind-hearted farmers took pity on the sobbing baron. They pushed and pulled him back into his fortress, dried his tears, and gave him some jam.

Baron de Bludge changed from that day on, having learned to say please. He became good, kind, friendly Baron de Bludge. He grew much thinner, and much happier, and everyone had a share of the strawberry jam.

ETHIOPIA

The Enchanted Princesses

There was a handsome young Ethiopian named Abeda, who took his rifle and went hunting. He wanted to catch a dibatag, which is a kind of gazelle. He had not seen one before, but he had heard they were wonderful creatures.

After much searching, he found five dibatags grazing quietly among some bushes. He raised his rifle, ready to shoot. Then he lowered it and looked at the dibatags again. He couldn't shoot them. They were too beautiful.

He quite fell in love with their beauty. They had pretty, slim bodies, and delicate legs, and long, graceful necks. Their faces were sweet and charming, and their wide, gentle eyes melted Abeda's very heart.

As they moved quietly about, they made him think of flowers and warm breezes, and other soft and perfect things.

"Oh, you dear Ethiopian beauties," whispered Abeda, overcome with love and admiration.

The dibatags heard him, but they didn't run away. They came towards Abeda, and gathered all round. They touched him with their noses, and smiled at him with their eyes.

Suddenly there was a great crashing in the bushes, and out charged another dibatag. He was a very angry dibatag, for he had his sharp horns pointed straight at Abeda!

There was no time to run. To save himself, Abeda raised his rifle and fired. Blam! Blam! He shot off the dibatag's horns!

The dibatag changed in an instant, into an ugly, angry djinn. He glared at Abeda for a moment, clutching his aching head. Then, without a sound, he disappeared.

Then, surprise on surprise! Round Abeda clustered five beautiful Ethiopian maidens! "Our hero," they sighed, stroking his shoulder. "You have broken the spell of the evil djinn who captured us and turned us into dibatags," they whispered, kissing his cheek.

The dibatags were really enchanted princesses all the time. No wonder Abeda fell in love at first sight of them!

The princesses led him back to their palace, where their unhappy family had been waiting a long time for them. There was great rejoicing, and everyone was so happy that they made Abeda a prince.

A wonderful banquet was held to celebrate. The princesses invited all their friends, and Abeda invited all his friends, including his four handsome brothers.

At the banquet, Abeda's brothers also fell in love with the beautiful princesses. So they married one each (Abeda married the prettiest princess) and they all lived happily ever after in their Ethiopian palace.

42

Liisa's Reindeer

Finland is a cold country in the very far north. In the coldest, most northerly part of all live the Lapps—the reindeer people.

Reindeer are their cows, for they give milk to the Lapps. Reindeer are their horses, for they pull sleighs and sledges for the Lapps. Reindeer are their wealth, for a rich Lapp is a man who owns many reindeer.

Liisa's father was a rich Lapp, for he had hundreds of reindeer. The best of his reindeer was Sulo. He was a very big fellow, with the most gigantic antlers you ever saw! He also had big, friendly eyes.

As soon as Liisa was big enough to ride by herself, her father gave her a beautiful little sleigh. It was the prettiest little one-girl sleigh there ever was. And Liisa's father gave her the great Sulo to pull her sleigh. They went everywhere together.

In the winter time, snow covers all Lappland. It lies on the ground, the trees, and even the frozen lakes. In the middle of winter, in December, the sun doesn't come to Lappland at all. Then the nights run into one another, with no daylight between them.

On one of those night kind of days, Liisa went fishing with her parents. Her father and mother rode in a big sleigh, pulled by four reindeer. Liisa went in her own little sleigh, with Sulo pulling it.

They rode right out on to a big lake, which was frozen as hard as the ground. Liisa's father chopped some holes through the ice, to reach the water. Liisa had her own fishing hole and her own fishing line. She even had her own stool to sit on, and a fur wrap round her, to keep off the cold air. She caught three fish!

"You shall have the biggest one to eat, as soon as we reach home," promised her mother. Then they climbed into their sleighs and set off across the lake again.

Suddenly, up came a great wind. It blew snow up from the ice, and more snow down from the clouds. It was so thick, and so dark, Liisa couldn't see her parents or their sleigh!

She was afraid, and called to them. She called as loud as she could, but she heard no answer. Sulo trotted on, through the blank whiteness. Liisa didn't know where they were. "I'm lost! I'm lost!" she sobbed.

Sulo stopped, and there was her father to lift her from her sleigh. She was back home!

"I thought I was lost!" she cried.

"Sulo wasn't lost," said her father. "He always knows his way home. That's why I gave him to you, to look after you."

Liisa stopped crying. She hugged her father and mother, and gave Sulo a big hug, too. Then they went indoors and cooked the fish. And Liisa ate two of them!

The Eiffel Tower

On a barge, on the River Seine, in France, lived a cat named Pierre. One day his barge stopped right in the middle of the city of Paris, close to the Eiffel Tower. Pierre tipped back his head. Way, way up near the top of the tower, he could see people standing on a platform. From there, so he'd heard, they could see all over Paris. He waved his tail to them, but no one waved back.

He tipped his head even more, and looked above the platform, at the Tower top. Something white fluttered there. Pierre stared and stared, but he couldn't make out what it was. It made him very curious, so he hopped off the barge and ran across to the Tower.

Pierre climbed the Eiffel Tower. He climbed for what seemed like hours. He had never thought there were so many steps in the whole world! When he finally reached the platform, he paused to take a rest. Then he looked down towards the ground.

"Yee-ow!" he cried, very surprised. Everything was so far away! Why, the river looked so small, he felt he could step right over it. And his barge was so tiny, he had to look hard before he even saw it!

Pierre sat, amazed and staring, for a long time. Then he remembered the mysterious whiteness he had seen at the very top of the Tower. So he continued his upward journey. Suddenly, the white thing fluttered round the corner of a girder, just ahead of him. Pierre rushed up and peeked round. It was a pigeon, just coming down to land on the tower.

Pierre was annoyed because he hadn't known it was a pigeon when he first saw it. Why, in his time he had seen—and chased—hundreds of pigeons. So Pierre did what he always did to pigeons. He pounced at this one. But he didn't land on his feet again. He landed on nothing. Pierre had jumped from the very top of the Eiffel Tower! Poor cat!

"Yee-owwwwww!" Down fell Pierre, down and down, till he was close to hitting the ground. But a dozen pigeons dived down after him. They caught him in their beaks—by the fur on his back, by his legs, and even by his tail! They set him gently on the ground.

Pierre thanked them very much, and then he ran home to his barge. He never climbed the Eiffel Tower again—and he never again chased pigeons, either!

GERMANY

In the Black Forest

In the south of Germany, near the River Rhine, is a place called the Black Forest. The hills there are covered with dark trees.

Hans lived in a small village, quite surrounded by the deep, dark forest. The villagers believed there were evil spirits, wicked witches and bad villains in the forest. "It's all right during the day," they all said. "But don't dare go into the forest at night!"

But Hans laughed at the stories. "If any strange creature is in the Black Forest, it's a good fairy. I'll prove it," he said.

So that night he took a lantern to light his way and set off through the forest. His friends begged him not to go, but Hans only laughed. Then he waved his hand to them, and walked off into the trees.

He strolled along, whistling a merry tune. Before long he came to a misty patch. "This mist smells strange and spicy," he said. Then he sat down on a rock and fell asleep!"

A huge, grey hand reached from the dark and pinched out the light in his lantern. Then it reached for Hans!

Flash! A good fairy, glowing with light, appeared between Hans and the grey hand. The hand drew back into the darkness.

"You cannot take this boy, because he believes in me," said the good fairy. You see, she had been hiding in the village that day, and she heard Hans talk about her.

An angry groan came from the darkness, and then the thing was gone.

The good fairy touched her magic wand to the lantern, and lit it again. She blew away the evil, strange-smelling mist. Then she hid where Hans would not see her.

Soon he woke, picked up his lantern, and sauntered on, whistling his merry tune.

He never knew anything of what happened while he slept. So he still does not believe there are evil things in the Black Forest.

GHANA

The Talking Cocoa Tree

John lived on a cocoa plantation in Ghana. He liked looking after the trees, and thinking of the lovely chocolate bars that could be made from the cocoa. He loved chocolate bars.

One day John saw that one of the trees was looking very poorly. All its leaves were drooping. "I wonder what's wrong with you," he said. He was really talking out loud to himself, for he never thought the tree could answer back.

But it did, which gave John quite a surprise! It said: "The ground here is full of rocks. I'm very thirsty, for the rocks won't hold any water for me to drink, like nice soft earth would."

John was very sorry for the tree. He brought a bucket of water and poured it over the ground. The tree roots sucked up as much as they could. "That's a bit better," said the tree. "But most of the water ran away out of my reach, because the rocks won't hold it."

John brought a spade and said, "Tell me where the rocks are, and I'll take them away from you."

The tree told John where to dig. He dug very carefully, and soon found the rocks. They were yellow rocks, and very heavy.

He lifted the rocks away from the tree's roots, and filled in the holes with nice, soft earth. "Aaaaah, that's better!" said the tree. Then John poured out some water for it. The tree drank it all up from the soft earth. Soon its leaves perked up again, and it looked about.

"Your kindness to me has made you rich," said the tree. "Those rocks are made of gold!"

John looked at the heavy yellow rocks again. What a surprise—the tree was right! He gathered up all the rocks, and took them to town, and sold them for lots of money.

And do you know what he spent it on? Lots and lots of chocolate bars!

The Goddess in the Sea

Constantine was a Greek fisherman who sailed the blue Aegean Sea. One day, as he was fishing, his net caught on the bottom.

He hauled hard on the net, but it was stuck fast. So he dived into the sea and swam down to see what it was caught on. He found a lovely statue, with the net wound round her hand. She seemed to be asking him to help.

"Poor thing," thought Constantine. "Left all alone and lonely on the bottom of the sea. I wonder how you came to be here." He swam back to his boat for a rope. He tied it round the statue and hauled her aboard his boat. Then he took her back to his home on the sea shore.

She looked rather sad and seaweedy, so he cleaned her until her white stone gleamed. Then he stood her in the sunshine in his garden.

Each day he went to look at her, and each day she seemed to smile more and more. "Ah, I knew she wanted the sunshine," said Constantine.

But then, day by day, her smile faded again. Constantine began to wonder if he hadn't given her too much sunshine. After all, she had spent a long time under the sea. Perhaps she missed the watery world down there.

Then Constantine realized who the lovely girl was! She was a statue of the old Greek goddess, Aphrodite. The goddess, so legend says, lived on the land and was the symbol of love and beauty. But she was born in the sea!

"Perhaps her statue needs the sea too," he said. Though he dearly wanted to keep the statue, so he could admire her beauty, he thought perhaps he should return her to the sea.

Then he had a wonderful idea. He moved the statue to a pool by the sea. When the tide came in, it covered her. Fish swam about her, and seaweed twined round her ankles. When the tide went out, she stood in the sun. Birds and butterflies played about her in the warm air.

The smile returned to the statue, and stayed there, under the water or in the sun. At last she was happy all the time. And Constantine was happy and contented too.

The Football Match

All through the winter the Greenland Eskimoes stay in their igloos. But when spring comes they pack their sledges, hitch up their husky dogs, and go to Smith Sound. They build whole new villages of igloos, they hunt the great walrus out of the frozen sea, and they play football. Village plays village, and everyone joins in—men and children, even women with babies on their backs.

The game starts halfway between two villages. Then everyone rushes at the ball and tries to kick it into the other side's village. They play very hard, and they play all day, until everyone is tired.

This is the amazing story of how a little boy called Patloq won a football match.

Patloq was the smallest player (not counting the babies). He played all day until he was very tired, and then he sat on the snow to rest. Then he saw that all the other players from his village were giving up too and falling down—just too tired to go on. Patloq jumped up, grabbed the ball, and started running as fast and as hard as he could. But he hadn't got very far when a man from the other side scooped him up, ball and all, and began to run in the opposite direction—towards *Patloq's* village!

"Help, help!" cried Patloq—but all his own team were too tired to help, and all the while they were getting closer and closer to Patloq's village. And then a wonderful thing happened. A great many-coloured thing swooped from the sky and lifted Patloq—and the ball, of course—right out of the man's arms. It carried him to the other village and set him down. Patloq had won the match!

Then the brilliantly coloured thing flew away.

Now Patloq has never heard of such a thing as a magic flying carpet, so he's still wondering what really happened to him.

But we know, don't we?

Miguel's Coffee

In Central America is a small country called Guatemala. It is full of mountains, many of them are volcanoes, but in the valleys there are many farms and many people.

This is the story of Miguel, who worked on a coffee plantation near Tajumulco, which is one of Guatemala's big fiery volcanoes.

Miguel loved growing coffee beans, because he loved drinking coffee. He drank so much coffee that his friends laughed at him.

But Miguel said: "My wife makes the best coffee in the world. What's more, it would quench any thirst!"

Well, just then the volcano, old Tajumulco, started to rumble. This frightened everyone very much. They thought he would erupt, and pour smoke and fire down on their heads.

So someone said: "It's too bad you don't have a big cup of coffee for old Tajumulco. It might put out *his* thirst!"

"What a good idea!" said Miguel.

He grabbed a bucket of coffee and ran to the top of the mountain.

Then he called out: "Hey, old mountain, you must be thirsty. Your breath is very hot, and when I look down your throat, I can see fire! Would you like some coffee?"

"Bellow!" went old Tajumulco. So Miguel poured the bucket of coffee down his throat.

Old Tajumulco gave a great gulp, and then he grew very quiet, and stopped pouring out smoke. The coffee had stopped his thirst!

Miguel went back down the mountain, and all his friends ran to tell him what a clever fellow he was! Then they had a party to celebrate. They ate coffee cake, and coffee flavoured chocolate, and coffee ice cream. And, to wash it all down—coffee!

GUINEA

Why Leopards Have Spots

Many, many years ago, when Africa was very wild indeed, a boy named Keita lived in Guinea in West Africa. Every day he would search for pretty pebbles in the rivers, and put them in a little leather bag. One day he found a lot of beautiful glossy brown pebbles, and he filled his bag with them.

Keita set off through the forest, to take his pebbles home. But he hadn't gone very far when he met a fierce leopard. Now in those days, believe it or not, leopards were just a plain golden colour all over.

This fierce leopard roared: "Goody! Here comes my dinner. A fat little boy!"

Keita didn't want to be eaten by the leopard. So he threw his bag of pebbles right into its mouth.

"Gulp!" said the leopard, swallowing the bag, with a very surprised look on his face. He tried to chase Keita. But with the pebbles inside him he couldn't run very fast.

Then the leopard saw a very strange thing. He was covered with lovely brown spots, where the pebbles inside him shone right through.

He was so pleased with the way he looked, he went to show himself off to all the other leopards. And they thought he looked so fine, *they* went and found some pebbles to swallow too.

And that's why leopards have spots.

The Giant Otter

Guyana is a hot country at the top of South America. It has lots of forests, rivers and mountains. Gold and diamonds, too!

George worked on the coast, on a sugar plantation. One day he thought: "I should like to be a rich man, and never work again. But I'll never get rich cutting sugar cane!"

So George left the coast and went inland to the valley of the Mazaruni River, to look for diamonds. They would make him rich!

It was a long, hard journey to the Mazaruni Valley. When he got there, George lit a fire, and made a cup of hot beef tea. It was too hot to drink at once, so he set it down to cool. Then he walked off for a bit, hoping to find some diamonds right away.

But he found no diamonds so he went back and picked up his cup. It was empty!

"Who drank my beef tea?" he cried.

"I did," said a voice. Out from behind a bush came a giant otter! He had short legs and a long body—seven feet from the point of his nose to the point of his tail! He had fine, silky fur all over his body, and a friendly smile all over his face.

"I couldn't help drinking your tea, it smelled so delicious," said the otter. "I'm sorry." George laughed. He didn't really mind the otter drinking his beef tea.

"You're very kind. Is there something I can do, to thank you for the tea?" asked the otter.

George laughed again. "I don't suppose you can find me some diamonds?" he asked.

"Yes I can!" replied the otter. "I know where there are lots of diamonds. But what good are diamonds to an otter?"

"I'll swap you!" cried George. "I'll swap beef tea for diamonds!"

"Agreed!" said the otter at once.

He took George to a place where diamonds littered the ground. George picked up so many, he filled a great sack with them.

The he made gallons of beef tea, and the otter drank it till he couldn't hold another drop. He just lay on his back, holding his bulging tummy, and smiling.

Now George is the richest man in the world. He lives in a castle, and wears silk socks and he's very happy.

But what of the otter? Is he left alone in the forest, with only the memory of beef tea? Oh, no! He went back to the coast with George. Now he lives in the castle, and drinks beef tea all day, and he's happy too.

How to Get Rid of a Giant

Haiti is a beautiful country on the island of Hispaniola, in the Caribbean Sea. Once upon a time, life was not very happy there, for a horrible giant terrorized the land.

He lived in the mountains, but whenever he was hungry he came storming down to steal food. He ate everything in sight, and if he was still hungry, he'd pull the roofs off the houses and steal the food inside. When he was full, he'd go back to the mountains, carrying a few banana trees over his shoulder, in case he got hungry on the way.

Well, the Haitians became very fed up with that giant. They didn't like growing food just for him to gobble. And they didn't like having to put their roofs back every other week. But they were scared of the giant, for he was ten times as big as anyone else.

So they decided to trick him. Next time he came down to raid them, everyone stood and laughed at him. "Ha, ha," they said. "Call yourself a giant? You may be good enough at pulling up trees by the roots. But if you were a *real* giant you could beat a hurricane."

When he heard that, the giant was so angry he could hardly wait till the next hurricane. When it came, he ran to the beach, where great waves were breaking, and the wind was tearing up trees by the dozen. The waves pounded the giant and swept over his head. But they couldn't shift him. The wind ripped away every tree in sight. But the giant wasn't moved.

Everyone was disappointed. They had hoped the hurricane would carry the giant away. But he was still with them, gorging their food and tearing up their houses. "We'll never be rid of him," they wailed.

Yet there was one clever boy, Pierre, who had seen that the giant never laughed. So he waited until he found a macaw asleep in a tree. He crept up to it and pulled out one of its long tail feathers.

He followed the giant up into the mountains, and waited till he fell asleep. Then he crept up to him and tickled the bottom of his foot with the feather. Now that mean giant had never once laughed, not ever. So all his laughter, which should have come out of him in bits and pieces all through his life, was still stored up inside him.

When Pierre tickled his foot, all the laughter in the giant swelled up and tried to come out of him all at once. But it couldn't, there was so much of it. So the giant just exploded with laughter. BOOM! he went. And then there was nothing left of him at all.

Humberto the Mule

Humberto was a mule who worked on a banana plantation in Honduras, Central America. On the way from the banana trees to the warehouse he carried two huge, heavy bunches of bananas, one on each side. On the way back to the trees, to pick up another load, he carried the big, fat, lazy mule driver.

Humberto didn't like carrying those great loads of bananas. Nor did he like carrying that great lump of a mule driver! The only thing he liked was eating bananas.

Whenever the mule driver was tired, he would lie down under a tree and go to sleep. Humberto didn't mind waiting, because that's when he got his chance to eat bananas. He reached his head round and bit a banana off his load. Then he laid it on the ground, and held one end of it with his foot. He peeled the skin off with his teeth, and ate the inside part.

Usually he only ate three or four bananas before the mule driver woke up. So the man didn't know what a clever banana-eating mule Humberto was. But one day he slept for hours and hours. Humberto ate seventy-seven bananas!

When the driver woke, he saw a pile of empty banana skins and a fat, happy mule. "Yi! What have you done?" he yelped. "Now I'll be in big trouble with my boss!" He grabbed a stick and hit Humberto!

Poor Humberto fell over—bump! and squashed one of his bunches of bananas to pulp. "Ai, ai! *Now* look what you've done!" screeched the driver, and went to hit Humberto again. Humberto jumped up to get out of the way. But he slipped on the mashed bananas and fell down again— squash! on the other bunch.

"Ai, ai, ai!" screamed the mule driver. But Humberto didn't wait to hear any more. He scrambled up and ran away. He didn't stop till he reached the city of San Pedro Sula.

He wandered round looking at all the sights of the city till he was hungry again. Then he discovered he still had one banana caught in the harness on his back. So he pulled off the banana, peeled it and ate it.

"What a clever mule!" said a voice. Humberto looked up, and there were dozens of children watching him. They all thought it was a wonderful trick for a mule to peel and eat a banana. They gave him more bananas and asked him to do it again.

Humberto still lives in San Pedro Sula, and a very happy mule he is. He has lots of friends there, and they all give him plenty of lovely bananas, and tell him what a clever mule he is.

52

HONG KONG

The Little Junk

Hong Kong is a tiny country off the coast of China. It has a fine, wide harbour, and ships come to it from all over the world.

A little junk named Son of the Moon lived there. He was a handsome little boat. His sails were the colour of moonlight, his decks were as white as snow, and his sides were a fine, bright red. Lee Kwan was his owner.

They worked in the harbour, carrying cargo from the big ships to the shore. Sometimes, Son of the Moon talked to the big ships. They told him tales of vast seas, strange cities, and all the places in the world.

Son of the Moon wished he could sail away to see all those wonderful things. But the big ships told him: "You're too small."

He asked Lee Kwan to take him travelling round the world. But Lee Kwan said: "You're too small, and the sea's too big."

But one night, when Lee Kwan went away and left Son of the Moon tied to the dock, he slipped his mooring rope and sailed away all by himself. "I'm going to see the world," he sang as he floated out to sea.

But, oh dear, when he reached the high sea, he didn't like it at all! The big waves knocked him about, and the fierce wind tore at his sails. "Help! Help!" he cried. Water was splashing into him. He was sinking!

Just then one of the big ships came past. A sailor threw down a rope. It looped round Son of the Moon's mast and held tight. The ship towed him back to Hong Kong.

Wasn't Son of the Moon glad to be back in his safe home again—and wasn't Lee Kwan glad to see him! He baled the water from Son of the Moon's hold, washed his sea-stained decks and mended his torn sails.

Then Son of the Moon was as bright and handsome as ever. But he never wanted to wander away from his home again.

Sour Grapes

Hungary is a country in central Europe. In that country lived a farmer who had a vineyard. His vines grew strong and lush, and they were loaded with enormous bunches of grapes. They looked wonderful, but they were the sourest grapes in the world. No one could eat them. They were so sharp and sour, they made people cry at the very first taste.

"These vines are useless!" growled the farmer. He brought an axe to chop them down.

"Stop!" cried a bird, who was sitting in the vines above the farmer's head. "It's not the vines' fault that their grapes are sour. It's your fault!"

"How can that be?" asked the farmer.

"Look around you," said the bird. "It's a sight to turn anything sour."

The farmer looked round. He looked at his little house, which had dirty walls and holes in its thatch. He looked at his three little girls, who sat crying in the dirty yard, with holes in their clothes and tangles in their hair. He looked at his angry wife screeching at the cat, the cat hissing at the mice, and the mice fighting each other. It *was* a sour sight.

"Sweeten your life," said the bird, "and your grapes will sweeten themselves."

So the farmer painted his house gleaming white, and put a fine new blue door on it. He thatched it with bright golden straw, and cleaned up the dirty yard. He bathed his children, combed their hair, and dressed them in pretty new clothes. He tickled his wife and made her laugh. Soon everyone was laughing. The cat sat in the sun and purred, and the mice played together under the vines.

The grapes grew sweet, and the bird sat in the vines and sang for joy.

The Eider Ducks

When you go to sleep, are you covered with duck feathers? If you have an eiderdown on your bed, then you are! You see, eiderdowns are filled with feathers from eider ducks.

These ducks live on the rocky shores of Iceland, which is a big, cold island in the North Atlantic Ocean. The Iceland farmers take the ducks' soft feathers, and sell them.

Do you think that's cruel, taking the ducks warm feathers? Well, it's not, for the ducks pull out their feathers themselves! Of course they don't do it to please the farmers—the mother ducks pull out their soft feathers to line their nests and keep their babies warm.

When the baby ducks are grown up, they leave their warm nests, and that's when the farmers take the feathers to make warm beds for us!

Once there was a greedy man who couldn't wait till the ducks had finished with their nests. One dark morning he took a sack to the place where thousands of ducks were nesting. He pushed a duck from her nest, and the baby ducks, too. Oh, how they shivered in the wind on the cold rocks! Their mother flapped and huddled over them as best she could, but she couldn't keep them warm

enough without her nest.

The greedy man stuffed the feathers in his sack and reached for the next nest.

But he never got to it!

For, at that moment the father ducks came back from catching fish to feed the mothers and babies. When they saw what the man was doing, they attacked him, skimming over the greedy man's head and bombing him with their fish. Hundreds of them.

Fish showered down on the man. Plop! Slither! Whack! Fish slid down his neck into his shirt. They filled his boots. When he put his hands over his head, they went up his sleeves!

"Yaaaaagh!" he cried. He dropped his sack, jumped in his boat, and rowed off howling. That was the last time he ever stole eider ducks' nests!

INDIA

The Neverending Feast

Once, long ago in India, there was a band of travelling musicians. They walked the roads, up and down the country, playing fine music.

They came one day to a great and beautiful palace. It belonged to the richest Rajah in the land, and he was having a feast that day. When he heard of the travelling musicians, the Rajah commanded them to play at his Feast.

The musicians tiptoed into the Rajah's great feast room. The walls were made of solid gold, and the ceiling was stuck all over with rubies and emeralds.

A thousand guests sat eating and drinking. They wore the finest clothes, and had so many jewels they could barely move. The Rajah was magnificent. His clothes were covered in diamonds. His hands were loaded with diamond rings, and the cup he drank from was made from a huge, glowing sapphire.

The musicians sat and played their sweet music for many hours, till the feast was ending. Then they asked the Rajah's servant to pay them so they could buy some food for themselves.

The servant laughed and laughed. "The Rajah never pays anyone. That's why he's the richest man in India!" he said. "Now go away."

The musicians were angry. They began to play a strange tune. The servant stopped laughing. He sat down and fell asleep. The musicians played to the Rajah and his guests. *They* all fell asleep where they sat. Soon the whole palace slept. Then the musicians went away.

All that happened many years ago. The musicians have disappeared forever. But the palace is still there, with the Rajah and all his guests still sleeping at their feast.

Carpet to the Rescue

Fatima and Shamsuzzakir spent a long time flying around Indonesia, because it is a place of many islands—big and small—and there were many things to see. The magic carpet flitted from island to island taking them on marvellous adventures.

One day they were flying over the sea, near an island. There were no beaches at that place—but steep cliffs rising from the sea. Suddenly, a little brown bird came whirling through the air and fell on the carpet. Fatima picked up the fluttering bird.

"Oh, she is frightened," said the girl. "I can feel her heart beating fast!"

"What's wrong, little swift?" asked her brother, who knew what kind of bird it was.

"The nest thieves have come!" squawked the swift. "Look!" She pointed her wing down at the sea. There was a small sailing boat, stopped beside the cliff. Men climbed from the boat, and disappeared into a cave in the cliff.

"My nest is in there! They've come to steal it! They'll take *all* the nests, and sell them to make soup!" wailed the unhappy bird. "Then where shall I lay my eggs?"

Now in that part of the world, soup made from swifts' nests is a great treat! But the birds who are robbed don't think so.

"We'll help you!" said Shamsuzzakir. He swished the carpet down into the cave.

It was a huge cave, full of screaming, zooming birds. The men paid no attention to the birds. They stood on bamboo ladders, knocking down the nests with sticks. The nests were stuck, like tiny white cups, high on the walls.

Shamsuzzakir flew the carpet past one of the men. He leaned out and shouted "Boo!" right in the man's face. What a fright it gave him! He slid right down his ladder.

They flew past another man. Fatima reached out and tickled him under the arm. He jumped from his ladder in a great hurry!

The carpet zipped round and round the cave, with the brother and sister making faces and playing pranks. The men were *so* frightened! They ran and jumped into their boat, and sailed away as fast as the wind would take them.

Fatima and Shamsuzzakir said goodbye to the happy swifts and flew away to look for more interesting adventures in other parts of the world.

IRAN

The Fish Who Cried

In the country of Iran is a very salty lake called the Lake of Rezaiyeh. The rivers and streams running into it are made of fresh water, but the lake is as salty as the sea. Now how did such a strange thing happen?

Long ago, when the lake was new, its water was quite fresh. Nearby lived a man who liked to eat fish, but there were none in the lake. So he set out on a long journey to the sea, and there he caught some baby fish. He put them in a big jar of water and carried them all the way home, put them into the lake, and spoke to them in this way: "Grow up, little fish, and multiply, and fill this lake with fish. Then I'll catch and eat you!"

Poor little fishes! They didn't want to be caught and eaten. They cried by night and they cried by day. But, as time passed, they grew up and in turn had little baby fish of their own. And the baby fish cried, too.

At last the man returned to the lake to catch some fish. He threw in a net and caught sixteen fish. They struggled and squirmed, but they couldn't get away. They struggled so hard, they splashed water over the man. Some of it hit his face, and went into his mouth.

It tasted salty! The man was so surprised, he took another taste of water. It really was salty. Then the man saw that the fish were crying. They had cried so much, their tears had turned fresh water to salt!

Then the man realized that the fish were unhappy. So he let them all go, and promised he would not catch them any more. The fish thanked him and swam away and they never cried again.

But, to this day, the waters of the Lake of Rezaiyeh are salty still.

Dougan's Donkey

Dougan harnessed his donkey to his cart and rode into town. He stopped outside Shaughnessy the grocer's, and went in to buy some food.

Along buzzed a bee and stung Dougan's donkey. "Yugh-ahh!" brayed the donkey. He lashed out with his hind feet, missed the bee, and kicked the cart to pieces.

Dougan's donkey rushed into Shaughnessy the grocer's, to show Dougan what had happened. He knocked over a crate of

apples and seventy-seven tins of baked beans.

Shaughnessy the grocer grabbed a broom and chased Dougan's donkey, shouting and sobbing with rage. Dougan followed, with his mouth hanging open and his hair standing on end, and never spoke a word.

Shaughnessy chased Dougan's donkey up the high street. The donkey ran into six cyclists and broke their bicycles. *They* took up the chase.

Dougan's donkey hid in Miss Felicity Finney's garden. Miss Felicity Finney popped out of her front door and whapped him on the head with her umbrella. The umbrella broke and Dougan's donkey ran on again. *She* took up the chase.

Up and down the high street they chased Dougan's donkey, who broke three fences, five shopping baskets, four windows and a whole cartload of milk bottles along the way.

At last they caught the donkey, and tied him to a big old tree in the square. Then they all turned and glared at Dougan.

"Pay for my groceries!" growled Shaughnessy.

"What about my lovely umbrella?" screeched Miss Felicity Finney.

"Your donkey's wrecked my bicycle!" shouted McFiggins, McFee, O'Shea, O'Sullivan, Lenihan and Flanagan, the cyclists.

Dougan just stood there, with his mouth hanging open and his hair standing on end, and never said a word. The donkey kicked and struggled to get away. Down fell the old tree!

Everyone scattered and ran to get out of the way of the falling tree. But Dougan just stood there, with his mouth hanging open and his hair standing on end, looking into the hole in the ground where the tree had been. It was full of gold coins—some old, buried treasure!

Dougan picked up the gold. He paid for everything his donkey had broken, and still had a sackful of gold left for himself. And he never said a word. He just laughed, and laughed.

ISRAEL

On the Kibbutz

Afri was a tiny, pretty gazelle who lived in the Negev Desert. The Negev is very hot and dry. It looks as if nothing could ever live there. But a few plants grow among the rocks and sand, so Afri could always find a mouthful to eat, here and there. Of course, he had to travel around quite a lot to find enough to eat.

One day he skipped down into a valley where he hadn't been for some time. He saw the most amazing thing—thick green grass, everywhere! He began eating the grass, and he ate until he was full. Then he lay down to give his stomach a rest.

Just then, a farmer came along. When Afri saw him, he jumped up and tried to run away. But he was so full of grass, he could only totter about. The farmer darted up and caught him.

He held Afri close, and said softly: "Don't be afraid. I won't hurt you." Then he took Afri back to his home, where he lived with lots of other farmers and their families.

"This is a kibbutz," he told Afri. "We all live and work together, to make a green farm in the desert. It's a very hard thing to do. But if a tiny fellow like you can live in the desert, then so can we!"

Everyone made a big fuss of Afri, and asked him to stay. "You can be our mascot," they said. So Afri stayed on the kibbutz, where he always had as much grass as he could eat.

59

The Pigeon on the Gondola

The city of Venice, in Italy, has canals instead of roads. People ride about in pretty gondolas, with gondoliers to row them.

Venice also has many pigeons. This is the story of the laziest pigeon in the whole city. He didn't care to fly if he could ride. So he would wait till Renzo's gondola came past, and hitch a ride on that.

One day Renzo lost his temper. "Get off my gondola, you lazy pigeon," he cried. "Why should I take you everywhere?"

The pigeon just cooed at him. So Renzo rocked the boat to make him fly away. The pigeon cooed louder. Renzo flung a cushion at him. The pigeon ducked and the cushion fell in the canal.

"Arrrgh! Look what you made me do!" shrieked Renzo. He swung his long, heavy oar at the pigeon—and nearly fell in the canal himself. He lay gasping in the bottom of the gondola.

The pigeon felt sorry for Renzo, so he made an offer to help him. At first Renzo was too angry to listen, but at last he agreed.

Now the pigeon still rides on Renzo's gondola. He holds flowers in his mouth, and gives one to each passenger. Everyone loves that, and wants to ride in Renzo's boat. So he's very busy and very happy. The pigeon is happy, too. All the passengers feed the pigeon and he's so fat he couldn't fly, even if he wanted to!

The Pygmy Hippo

The African country called the Ivory Coast has much more than a coast. There's a lot of country, and much of it is forest.

In the deepest forest was a pygmy hippopotamus. He was quite a young pygmy hippo, for he had just left his mother and set out to live on his own. He wandered through the forest, muttering to himself. "I don't see why I couldn't stay at home. Mother says pygmy hippos always live on their own. But *I* don't like it. *I'm* lonely. I wish I had some company."

He came to a stream with high muddy banks. "Ho, hum," he said. "This is the right sort of place for a pygmy hippo to live."

So he found a place in the bank where there was a little cave facing the water. It was just the right sort of place for a pygmy hippo. "Ho, hum," he said. "I suppose I'd better get to work." He dug away at the cave, until he'd made it nice and deep. Then he crawled in.

"Now I'm invisible. I can hide here and no one can see me," he said. "That's just what Mother told me to do. It's the kind of cave she lives in. It's the kind of cave *all* pygmy hippos live in. I guess I should be happy." But he wasn't. He was too lonely.

Also, he wasn't a very good cave-maker. Because, while he sat in his cave, a duiker walked on the bank above it. She was only a little duiker, just a small antelope. She didn't weigh much. Tip-tap went her little feet over the top of the cave. Sludge, slollop! The bank fell into the water.

"Help! Help!" cried the duiker, struggling in the muddy water.

"What? What's up? Or down?" cried the pygmy hippo, struggling out from under his roof.

He saw the duiker. He *hurled* himself into the water, and pushed her back to shore.

"Oh, thank you," said the duiker. "What a big, strong fellow you are!"

"Me? Big and strong?" said the surprised pygmy hippo. "I'm a tiny little *pygmy* hippo!"

"Perhaps you are," said the duiker, "but to me you're a big, strong fellow."

The pygmy hippo felt very proud of himself then. He puffed out his chest, and snuffled happily.

Now, every evening when the duiker comes to the stream to drink, the pygmy hippo comes out of his cave. He watches to make sure she doesn't fall in the water. Then they have a little chat, and he isn't lonely any more.

The Golden Rayed Lily

In the city of Tokyo, on the island of Honshu, in the country called Japan, a beautiful child once lived. She was so bright and lovely that she was called Sun Blossom.

From the windows of her home, Sun Blossom could see, a long way across the Plain of Tokyo, to Mount Fuji. She asked her mother about it.

"Once it was a volcano," said her mother. "It was full of fire, and it threw out burning stones that covered the ground, and thick smoke that filled the air. But it's just a mountain now with snow on top."

"But the top of the mountain is blue!" said Sun Blossom. "It can't be snow!"

"Yes, it's snow," said her mother. "It looks blue sometimes when the sun shines on it."

Sun Blossom didn't understand that. How could white look blue when the sun shone on it?

The next time she saw Mount Fuji, its top was coloured grey. Another day it was mauve. And then, one day, it shone like gold! Seeing that, Sun Blossom was sure that her mother must be wrong. "It can't be snow!" she thought. She longed to see what it really was.

And so she left her home, and set off to walk to the mountain. She walked many hours and many miles to reach Mount Fuji.

At last, as the sun was setting, she came to the foot of the mountain and looked up. The top was glowing pink, the most beautiful colour she had ever seen.

Sun Blossom began to climb the mountain. It grew dark and cold, and still she climbed, tired though she was.

When morning came, Sun Blossom saw the sun shine once more on the wonderful top of the mountain. It shone bright, in all the colours of the rainbow. She laughed for joy, and ran on till she stood upon the beautiful colours.

But, oh, it was cold and wet! And when she looked more closely, Sun Blossom saw that it really was snow on the top of Mount Fuji. And it *was* white, though it shone so colourfully.

Unhappy Sun Blossom was so weary and cold and disappointed, that she couldn't walk another step. She fell down in the snow and it covered her like a soft blanket. She slept, and she slept, until she died.

Her sad parents searched everywhere for her, and never found her. But on the spot where she had died, a gorgeous lily grew. It was white and gold and rose, just like the snow when the sun shines upon it.

The sorrowing mother and father took it, and planted it in their garden. They called it their Golden Rayed Lily, in memory of Sun Blossom. Now lilies like that grow all over Japan, and in gardens everywhere.

The Kind Old Bus

In Jordan was an old bus who carried people between the country and the town. He also took their loads of sesame, grapes, olives and dates, all packed on his roof. He was a friendly old bus, and everyone loved him. Except his driver, Bashir.

Bashir said the bus should stop only at proper bus stops. He said it should always be on time, to the dot, by his big silver watch. But the bus stopped himself wherever he pleased, to let the people on and off.

This made Bashir wild with anger.

One day a bent, tottery old man, with a great heavy pack, was on the bus. "Will you take me right up to my house?" he politely asked Bashir.

"No, no!" cried Bashir. "Your house is on the wrong road. We must stay on this road."

"But it's as hot as the desert today!" cried the old man. "It's too hot for walking!"

The bus stopped himself. "Let's take the old man to his house," he said to Bashir.

The passengers shouted at Bashir. "Go to the old man's house. We don't mind!"

Bashir was very angry at the bus. He jumped out. "If you won't do as I say, I won't drive you any more," he screeched.

But the bus drove off, all by himself, to the old man's house! At first the passengers were a bit scared, riding without a driver. But the bus drove himself very well, and took them all to their houses.

So everyone was very pleased and happy with the kind old bus. Except Bashir, who had to hitch a ride home on a camel!

63

The Zebra's Stripes

In the country of Kenya, on the eastern side of Africa, are wide, grassy plains. This is the home of great herds of zebras.

Zebras didn't always have stripes. Once there were two kinds of zebras—black ones and white ones. The black zebras were very proud of their fine, shining colour. They thought they were the most beautiful animals ever! Strangely enough, the white zebras thought exactly the same about themselves.

But lions, and men, and other assorted zebra hunters, didn't mind in the least what colour a zebra might be. They chased and caught them all the time, they were so easy to see!

At last the zebras became desperate about the situation. "There soon won't be any zebras left at all," they said.

So, black and white, they gathered to discuss their problem. They thought of running away, but there would be hunters wherever they went. They thought of hiding in the mountains, but then they would have no grass to eat.

A white zebra spoke up. "There's one way we can hide, right here. I've noticed," he said, "that when a white zebra stands under a tree, the shadows of the branches make black stripes on him. He's very hard to see like that."

Saved from the Storm

Riding on their magic carpet, Fatima and Shamsuzzakir arrived over Korea just as a violent storm struck. It rained so hard, they were soaked in a moment.

The carpet saved them. It rolled itself up tight, with Fatima and Shamsuzzakir inside. Then it plunged down to earth.

Bump! They landed right up against the door of a little mud house. The house had a straw roof, with rope nets holding it down.

A man opened the door to see what the noise was, and the carpet jumped right into his arms! Clutching the carpet the man staggered back into the house where his wife and children helped him to unroll it. Out popped Fatima and Shamsuzzakir!

Everyone thought it was all very funny. Soon they were good friends.

The Koreans gave them a lovely meal, of rice and shrimps and peaches. Then they saw that the storm had finished, and the sun shone.

Before they left, Fatima and Shamsuzzakir gave the children a ride on the magic carpet.

"Do you mean we should cover ourselves with black stripes?" asked the angry white zebras.

"And we should put white on our beautiful black coats?" asked the black zebras.

"That's right," said the white zebra.

Well, well, what a muttering and complaining came from every zebra! But none of them could think of a better plan.

So every black zebra gave some of his colour to a white zebra. The white zebras gave some of theirs. Then they looked at one another.

"Why, aren't we handsome!" they cried.

So the zebras were pleased with their new look. And they were even more pleased to find they were now much harder for hunters to see.

LAOS

The Beautiful Pagoda

In the Kingdom of Laos, in South East Asia, is the city of Louang Prabang. This is the City of One Hundred Pagodas.

A long time ago, there was a king in Louang Prabang who wanted to build a wonderful pagoda. He wanted it to be even more beautiful than any other pagoda.

One day the king was striding up and down in his garden, talking and muttering to himself about his problem.

"Please excuse a humble gardener speaking to you, Your Majesty," said a gardener. "The answer is right here before your eyes!" The gardener pointed to a parakeet in a tree.

"You're right!" cried the king as he looked at the bird. For the parakeet was dressed in the most beautiful greens, golds, reds, yellows and blues.

The king called for his architects and builders and showed them the parakeet. "Make my pagoda in the colours of that bird," he commanded.

They did, and it's the most beautiful pagoda in the City of One Hundred Pagodas.

The Little Giant

The Lebanon is a small, crowded country at the eastern end of the Mediterranean Sea. Thousands of years ago, when there were fewer people in the world, giants lived there. But the land slowly filled up with ordinary-sized people. There wasn't enough room for the giants then, so they moved away. They went to the large, remote and hidden lands, where there was room for them. Since then no one has seen them.

At the top of one of Lebanon's rocky mountains was a big cave. No one knew it was there, for it was blocked up with stones. Then one day the stones began to move. They tumbled away from the cave and bounced down the mountain. There was a little giant in the cave, and she wanted to come out. So she pushed them out of her way.

She was a little girl giant named Sharon. She had slept in the cave for ten thousand years, under the spell of a wicked sorcerer.

He hid her in the cave, and went away, and no one ever knew she was there!

But now, at last, Sharon was awake. Poor child, she didn't know the other giants had gone away. She didn't know the land was filled and teeming with millions of ordinary-size people! She began to walk down the mountain, looking for some other giants. Crash, smash went her feet through the land. She trod on trees as you would tread on grass!

Then she heard a tiny squeaking, coming from near her foot. She looked down, and a man cried, "Don't step on me!"

He was an ordinary-sized man, but to Sharon he was so small, she could hardly see him. Why, he stood only as high as her ankle! She picked him up, and held him gently, and asked him where the other giants were.

"Why, they all left here many, many years ago," he said. "Nobody knows where they've gone, but they must be somewhere."

At that news, Sharon shed a tear. It was a little tear to her, but it happened to fall on the man, and it soaked him to the skin!

Then she looked about, and saw how crowded the land was. "I can't stay here," she said, "for everyone is so small, I'm afraid I might step on them. I shall go and look for all the other giants."

So the man led her through the country. He showed her the best places to put her feet, where she wouldn't hurt anyone. At last they came to the Mediterranean Sea.

"Goodbye," said she. And without another word the sad little giant swam away, to search in all the lost, faraway places of the world for the other giants.

The Shepherd's Pancakes

Matete was a shepherd boy. He lived in Lesotho, a country in Africa.

Matete spent all his days on the mountain slopes, herding his sheep. It was a very hard life, for he sometimes lost some sheep. They were forever straying away.

Each evening, when Matete went home, his father counted the sheep. He scolded Matete whenever another sheep was lost, and told him he was a bad shepherd. That made Matete very sad, for he really wanted to be a good shepherd.

He thought of a way to stop his sheep from straying. He bought a frying pan.

Are you wondering: "Whatever use is a frying pan for herding sheep?"

Ah, but clever Matete knew that sheep are curious. They always like to see what's going on. So he put on a show for them. He made pancakes, over a little campfire, every day.

To make pancakes, you put batter in a frying pan and cook it. When the first side is done, you turn it over and cook the second side. But Matete didn't turn his pancakes in an ordinary way. He tossed them!

Here's how he did it: When a pancake was half cooked, he gave the pan a twitch. The pancake rose in the air, turned over, and fell back in the pan upside down!

"Baaa! Baaa!" bleated the watching sheep. That's their way of saying: "Oh, good show!"

Sometimes Matete tossed his pancakes in fancy style. He made them spin over and over, high in the air, before catching them again. He could even send a pancake soaring over his head, and catch it behind his back!

Matete never lost any more sheep, for they always stayed close to watch his pancake show. His father was very pleased and told everyone: "My son is the best shepherd in Lesotho!"

He was also the fattest shepherd in Lesotho, from eating all the pancakes!

The Happy Tribe and the Slave Traders

Liberia is a small country, on the Atlantic edge of Africa. A long time ago, before it was called Liberia, it was a very wild place. But it wasn't empty of people. Many tribes lived in the forests.

One of these was called the Happy Tribe. They had the gift of laughter. Wherever they went, the forest filled with merriment. They smiled at the sun and they danced in the rain. Through the great forests they wandered, living joyfully on the fruit of the land.

One day they met another tribe, rushing through the forest and wailing with fear. "Wicked strangers have come from across the sea," they told the Happy Tribe. "They're catching everyone they see. They tie them up, and put them on their ship, and carry them away. They sell them for slaves in a far country. And the poor slaves never come back!" Then the frightened ones hurried away.

The Happy Tribe were sad for a while, but they never thought that *they* might be caught! So they were taken quite by surprise when the wicked slave traders attacked them one day.

Then the Happy Tribe was happy no more. The wicked men marched them through the forest. They were heading for the sea, and the terrible slave ship! The poor captives wept, and pleaded to be let free. The wicked men only laughed, and made them march faster than before.

But when the wicked men were asleep, one boy wriggled from his ropes. He crept up to the sleeping man who had a knife in his pocket. The boy stole the knife without waking him, and crawled back to the captives.

All the Happy Tribe watched him hopefully. The boy cut their ropes, taking care not to make any noise. Then they all tiptoed softly away.

By morning they were miles away, and though the wicked ones searched, they didn't find them.

After that, the Happy Tribe were very careful and watchful. They kept away from the coast where the slave traders lurked, and were never caught again. And though their adventure taught them to cry, they never forgot how to laugh.

LIBYA

The Mysterious Cave

Mustafa lived the nomad life in Libya, which is a dry country in the north of Africa. Being a nomad meant he never stayed anywhere very long. His family was always moving on, to find new pastures for their cattle.

One day Mustafa found a kitten, alone and deserted. It was a wild Sand Cat kitten. Mustafa fed it on cow's milk, and kept it for a pet.

But one day, the kitten jumped from Mustafa's arms and ran away. Everyone was in a hurry, for they were passing through a very dry place where there was no grass or water for the cattle. They left the kitten and hurried on.

But Mustafa ran into the rocks. At first he couldn't find the kitten anywhere. Then he saw its footprints leading into a small hole in a wall of rocks. He crawled after it, and came into a cave. It was big and dark.

He saw two eyes glinting above him. "Caught you!" he cried. He reached out for his kitten, but what he touched was stone!

How odd! Mustafa peered into the dark. Then he saw that the eyes were made of beautiful green stones. Emeralds, perhaps! They were the eyes of a carved stone cat! What was it doing in the cave? Was it guarding a treasure?

"Miaow!" said a voice. Mustafa jumped with fright, but it was his kitten, not the statue!

Mustafa picked up his kitten and ran from the cave to catch up with his family, who were already miles ahead. But he promised himself that someday he would go back to discover the mystery of the stone cat with the emerald eyes.

LUXEMBOURG

The Land of Fairy Tales

A long time ago an unhappy musician lived in Luxembourg. He was unhappy because no one liked his music. When he played his piano, they all groaned and made faces. When he played his violin, they clapped their hands over their ears and begged him to stop. And when he played his trumpet, they threw rotten cabbages at him.

Poor, unhappy, lonely musician! He wandered the whole country, hoping to find someone to listen to him. But all the people he met rudely told him to stop his horrible noise. Birds flew away, rabbits ran underground, and even the fish swam up waterfalls to get away from the sound of him.

At last the musician could stand it no longer. He sat down and wept. And then, quite suddenly, he felt someone softly wipe away his tears. He stopped crying and looked up, and there was the Spring wind.

"Don't cry, little musician," she whispered. "Come and play your trumpet for me. I'll show you how."

And she scooped him up and carried him up to the top of a hill.

There she sat him down, and she taught him to blow his trumpet. All through the Summer he learned to play sweet and lively. All through the Autumn he learned to play quiet and sad. All through the Winter he learned to play hard and strong. Then the Spring wind picked him up and drifted down the hill into the town of Luxembourg.

Sitting in her arms, the musician played his trumpet soft and sweet, warm and low. The sound of his playing brought everyone into the streets.

"Spring's here!" they all said happily. "Listen, you can hear it!"

The musician smiled to himself and played the prettiest tune anyone had ever heard, for he was happy at last. He didn't mind that the people could not see him. Because now they liked his music, and that was all he had ever wanted.

MADAGASCAR

The Muddy Ox

Jacques was a young ox who lived in a grassy green field on a farm in Madagascar. One day the farmer came and led him to a rice field which was flooded with water. Jacques didn't want to go in. "I'll get all wet and muddy!" he cried.

"That's what you're supposed to do," said the farmer. "You have to walk round and round in the water, till it gets thick and muddy. Then I can plant more rice in it."

Well, Jacques didn't like it at first, all that tramping round in the sticky mud. But soon he found what fun it could be! He ran round and round, splashing water, covering himself with mud, and having a lovely time.

Then the farmer took him back to his field, but Jacques didn't like it any more. He wanted to play in the mud. So, the moment he had a chance, he went back to the rice field.

Oh, what an uproar! The farmer had planted more rice there, and silly Jacques was kicking it all out. The farmer chased Jacques from the rice field.

Jacques felt very upset, so he ran away to the forest. But he didn't like *that* very much because there was no grass to eat.

Then he met a sunbird—a pretty blue and yellow fellow—who was drinking nectar from a flower with his long, sharp bill. "Please," said Jacques, "can you tell me my way home?"

"If you could fly like me, you could see over the trees and you'd soon find your way," said the sunbird. But he very kindly flew up, spotted the farm, and told Jacques the way to go.

Jacques hurried home and lived happily ever after in his grassy field. He never went back to the forest. But sometimes—and only when the farmer asked him—he went to the rice field to play in the mud!

MALAWI

Fire Alarm!

Fatima and Shamsuzzakir were flying over Africa on their magic carpet. When they came to the land of Malawi, they saw a brush fire burning through the grass. All the animals were running away and crossing a stream, where the fire couldn't follow them. A mother cheetah jumped across, carrying a kitten in her mouth. Then she turned and ran back towards the fire.

Fatima and Shamsuzzakir saw her run towards three more kittens. She picked up one and headed for the river. "Ooo," said Fatima. "We must save the other kittens!"

So Shamsuzzakir steered the magic carpet down, and Fatima snatched up the kittens.

They flew so fast, they crossed the stream and put down the kittens even before the mother cheetah arrived. And wasn't she surprised to see them there, safe and sound!

The Cheeky Little Tailorbird

In Malaysia, on the island of Borneo, lived a cheeky tailorbird. She made her nest, as all tailorbirds do, by sewing together two long leaves.

She needed thread for her sewing, so she stole it from the silkworms. This annoyed them, for they were trying to build their cocoons with it. "Go away," they shouted at her—as loudly as silkworms *can* shout.

But she chirped back: "Don't shout at me, you silly worms, or I'll eat you all up!"

She frightened the silkworms so much, they crawled away and hid in dark holes and corners.

"*Now* how shall I finish my nest?" she said, very annoyed with the silkworms. Then she remembered a big spider, who had a huge web.

The spider was sitting in his web, minding his own spider business. Along came the tailorbird and nipped off a strand. "Hey!" shouted the angry spider—as loudly as a spider *can* shout.

"Don't shout at me, you horrible spider, or I'll eat you up!" cheeped the tailorbird.

She frightened him so much, he ran off and built a new web, where she couldn't find him.

So the tailorbird used the rest of his old web to finish sewing up her nest. She filled it with down, which she took from seed pods. At last there was only one more thing to do, before she could lay her eggs.

"I need some hairs to make a really soft bed for my chicks," she said. She flew about till she found an orang-utan dozing in a tree. Ping! The cheeky tailorbird pulled a hair right from the top of his head!

"Yowch!" cried the orang-utan, waking up fast. Quick as a flash, he reached out a long arm and caught the tailorbird.

"Owowowowowowow ! ! !" screamed the cheeky tailorbird. "My poor children!" she sobbed.

"What do you mean?" said the puzzled orang-utan. "You don't *have* any children!"

"Of course not," she snapped. "I can't have children till I've finished my nest. And I can't finish my nest till you let me go!"

This confused the orang-utan so much, he let the tailorbird go, and she flew away to put the hair in her nest. So, if you're ever in Borneo, keep your hat on! The cheeky tailorbird is looking for hair!

Bring Back the Oxpeckers

Long ago in a village in Mali, in Africa, all the cattle were plagued with ticks. These are horrid insects which live in the animals' hides, and make them very miserable indeed, by biting them. The Dogons were at their wits' end. "What can we do?" they cried. "What have we *done,* that our cattle should be so plagued?"

"You chased away the oxpecker birds. *That's* what you did!" said an old wise woman.

"But the oxpeckers were nesting in our roofs!" said the men. They didn't like the oxpeckers making holes in their thatches. So, the year before, they had chased the birds away.

But now they listened to the old woman's wise words. They went out of the village and called across the land: "Oxpeckers! Oxpeckers, come back! There is need of you here! You may nest in our roofs, and we won't chase you!"

Soon oxpeckers were flying in from all directions. They nested in the roofs, and they took away the ticks from the cattle.

How did they do it? Why, how do you suppose oxpeckers got their name? By riding about on animals' backs, and eating the ticks!

Now everyone in the village is happy. Except the ticks.

73

MALTA

The Brave Knight

Malta is a small island in the Mediterranean Sea. Centuries ago, it belonged to the Knights of St John. They had rich castles and palaces, churches and hospitals there.

There were also villainous, thieving pirates on the sea in those days. Very clever pirates they were, too. They waited until the knights were away from the island on a crusade. Then they sailed up and stole the treasure from the castles and palaces.

But there was one knight left on the island. He was a very new knight, little more than a boy. It was young Sir Royston Greer.

When the pirates attacked, Sir Royston was on the other side of the island. A frightened villager brought the news to him.

"Zounds!" cried Sir Royston. He jumped on his great horse, and raced away.

He arrived on the scene just as the pirates, loaded with all the things they had stolen, were climbing down a cliff. Waiting at the bottom was their ship.

Did brave Sir Royston attack the pirates, regardless of odds? No, *clever* Sir Royston did not! Instead he pushed a great rock from the cliff top. Crunch! The rock went straight through the decks and bottom of the ship. With a gurgle the ship filled with salt-water and quickly sank, like the rock.

The pirates were trapped. They couldn't go down, for there was nothing below them but the deep sea. They couldn't go up, for at the cliff top stood Sir Royston, with his shiny armour, his lance, and his sword.

Sir Royston made them come up, one at a time. He kept guard while the villagers tied them up. He took all the treasures, and put them back where they belonged. And all the pirates were put in prison, till they learned it wasn't safe to take on brave, clever Sir Royston Greer!

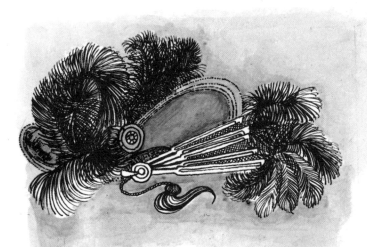

MAURITANIA

Farid's Fine Farm

Mauritania is a dry country in Africa. Much of it is a completely waterless desert—the Sahara Desert. Much is almost-desert. But in one tiny corner, along the Senegal River, there are farms.

Farid had a farm there. Well, he really had only one small field. One day he stood looking at his field. "I wish I had a bigger farm," he said to himself.

A passing stranger overheard Farid, and he laughed out loud. "*My* land is five hundred times larger than yours," he said to Farid. "But I would trade with you."

Farid was such a greedy young man, he wanted to trade without asking questions. Silly fellow. So they shook hands, and the trade was settled.

Farid set off eagerly for his new land. But when he arrived—oh, my! His fine new property was almost in the desert. All that grew there, near a small puddle of an oasis, were a few bits of grass and three date palms. The only other living things for many miles around were some ostriches.

Then Farid saw what a silly, greedy fellow he had been, to trade his good field for this! Nothing would ever grow there. And then he thought of something! So he built himself a house under the palms, and made friends with the ostriches.

It's not easy to make friends with ostriches. They're very big, but very shy birds. And they can run very, very fast. But Farid didn't run after them. He coaxed the ostriches to come to him, by giving them shiny stones to eat! And that wasn't a cruel thing to do. For ostriches are *always* swallowing stones. They keep them in their stomachs to help grind up their food. In fact they'll swallow anything, especially bright things—from watches to bottle tops.

Farid made friends with the ostriches because he wanted the beautiful, long white feathers from their wings and tails. People use them to decorate hats and fans.

The ostriches were soon such good friends with Farid, they let him pull out their feathers. And *that* wasn't cruel, either, because he didn't pull the feathers until new ones were ready to grow in their place.

Farid took all the lovely feathers to town, and sold them for a high price. And so he had a good farm after all. He had the best ostrich feather farm in all Mauritania!

The Roadrunner

Maria was a Mexican schoolgirl. She was the best runner in her whole school. She won all the school prizes for running.

"Maria, you're a good runner," her teacher said. "But you must practice and become a *very* good runner. Then you can win races against the best runners from other schools."

So Maria practised running. Every morning she ran from her home in the country to her school in the town. Each afternoon, she ran home again.

But one day, halfway home, she stopped. "How can I race when there's no one to race with? No one can run as fast as I can," she said.

"Not true," croaked a roadrunner bird, skipping out from behind a bush. "*I'll* race you!"

Perhaps you've never met a roadrunner bird, so I'll tell you about them. They are very bad at flying, but wonderful at running!

"All right, let's race!" cried Maria. Away she ran in a cloud of dust. And at her feet, in his own cloud of dust, ran the roadrunner.

They raced all the way to Maria's house, and the roadrunner won. "Let's race again tomorrow," said Maria. "Perhaps I'll win then."

So the next day they raced, and the next, and the next. But the roadrunner always won.

Maria didn't mind. Perhaps she couldn't run as fast as a roadrunner bird, but she could beat any other girl runner in the country.

And she did.

Carpet Magic

Along the southern coast of France flew the magic carpet, bearing Fatima and Shamsuzzakir. They were looking for tiny Monaco.

Zip! They flew right over it in just two seconds.

"Turn back!" cried Fatima. "We've gone straight past it!" The magic carpet obediently circled round and sailed, low and slow, over the country. They passed a great rock, sticking out into the sea, where the Prince of Monaco lives in a palace.

Suddenly Shamsuzzakir pointed out to sea. "Look!" he called. "A boat in trouble."

Without waiting for orders, the carpet turned and dashed over the sea. There was a boy in a very old, leaky rowing boat. It was filling with water. He baled out the water as hard as he could go. But the boat was still sinking.

Shamsuzzakir pulled off his Persian sash. He threw one end to the boy. "Catch hold," he shouted, "and we'll tow you to shore."

The boy grabbed the sash. Shamsuzzakir held tight to his end, and Fatima steered the carpet for the beach. They flashed along, towing the old boat so fast, it looked like a dashing speedboat. But still it sank, lower and lower in the water.

When they were thirty yards from shore, it sank. "Hold on!" shouted Shamsuzzakir. The boy held fast to the sash and they carried him through the air to the beach. He looked like someone on a trapeze!

The carpet slowed and lowered him gently to the sand. Then it landed beside him.

"Thank you very much, whoever you are," said the boy. "Are you magicians?"

"No, but our carpet is magic," said Fatima.

"Oh, that's too bad," said the boy. "I hoped you could return my poor old boat from the bottom of the sea for me."

Now, the magic carpet said not a word. But, as usual, it knew everything that was going on. And do you know what it did? It

brought the old boat out of the sea by magic. It popped up through the waves and floated back to the beach!

And the carpet's magic didn't stop there. Oh no! For it made the old boat as good as new, with never a leak in its shiny planks.

Fatima and Shamsuzzakir were as surprised as the boy, for their carpet had never done anything like that before!

But they patted it, and told it what a good, clever carpet it was. The carpet rippled and gleamed its colours with pleasure. Then it carried them off to a new adventure.

The Little Wild Horses

Once, long ago, a Prince of faraway Mongolia made a law about animals. "One horse is now worth one ox, one yak, half a camel, seven sheep or fourteen goats," he decreed.

Up spoke a little horse. "I'm worth more than *half* a camel! I'm worth a *whole* camel, all by myself!" he said with great pride.

The oxen, yaks, sheep and goats laughed at the angry horse. The big camels sneered. The Prince told his soldiers to cut off the little horse's head for daring to answer back!

But the little horse kicked the Prince's tent over his head, and ran so fast, not even the long-legged camels could catch him. He ran to the farthest faraway part of Mongolia. On the way, he told other horses of the Prince's new law. They didn't like it either, so they went with him.

The Prince sent searchers, but they never found the horses. So, to this day, the little wild horses of Mongolia live in the most faraway parts of the country.

MOZAMBIQUE

The Runaway Train

A little railway engine came to live in Mozambique. While he was being made he was just parts and pieces. But when the fire was lit in his boiler, he came alive.

He was in the city of Mocambique, beside the Indian Ocean. He sat looking at it for a while. Then his driver climbed aboard.

"Let's go," said the driver, and off they went. They huffed through orange groves and forests. They puffed up hills and through cane fields.

The young engine loved every minute of the trip. He could hardly wait to do it again.

So back and forth he went, enjoying all the sights. But after he had seen the same things hundreds of times, he grew bored.

"Let's go somewhere else for a change," he said. "Let's go to Lake Nyasa."

The driver laughed. "We can't go to Lake Nyasa! Our lines don't go that way."

But the little engine wasn't worried about that. "I can run without lines," he said.

The driver only laughed, and wouldn't

MOROCCO

The Startled Starlings

Mr and Mrs Fenzar lived in a village in Morocco, and Mr Fenzar had some fig trees.

One day he rose long before sunrise. He was just hurrying out the door when Mrs Fenzar stopped him: "I want you to fix my kitchen ceiling today. There is a huge crack in it and I'm afraid it will fall down!"

"I'm sorry, I can't fix it today," said Mr Fenzar. "I must pick my figs, before the starlings eat them!" He hurried away.

That same day Mrs Fenzar was cooking his dinner when, with a crack and a crash, down came the ceiling! It fell on Mrs Fenzar's head, and into Mr Fenzar's dinner.

Mrs Fenzar burst into tears. She threw the ruined food out the door, she was so angry.

A flock of starlings saw the food and flew down to eat it. But their first bites were lumps of plaster, and the second bites were so hot, they burned their tongues. "Gah!" they cried, and flew off to the fig orchard.

In the orchard were many more starlings. They were eating the ripe figs and laughing at Mr Fenzar. No matter what he did or shouted, he couldn't scare off those greedy birds.

"Fly! Fly for your lives!" cried the first starlings. "There's a wily woman in the village who tricked us terribly. Fly away, before she pulls any more tricks on us!"

The starlings flew off in a panic. Mr Fenzar cheered to see them go: "My figs are saved!" Then he went home to find Mrs Fenzar covered in plaster dust, and crying.

Mr Fenzar dried her tears and dusted her down. He cleared away the mess and put up a new ceiling. Then everyone was happy—except the starlings, who never dared to return again.

go. So, one day when the driver got off at a station, the engine ran away. He jumped clear off the tracks, and trundled into the forest. He was going to Lake Nyasa!

But there were no shining lines ahead to point where he should go. Soon the little engine was lost. His fire went out.

Really, he wasn't lost at all, for his driver had been running behind. He caught up to the little engine. He scolded him, then he re-lit his fire, and took him back.

The little engine stays on the lines these days, and never tries to run away. But he still wants to see Lake Nyasa.

MUSCAT AND OMAN

The Sultan and the Sun

In a time long gone, a wicked sultan ruled the sunny kingdom of Muscat and Oman. This wicked sultan was also a very vain and silly man. He even thought the sun shone only at his bidding.

Every morning he rose early from his bed, before the sun was up. His slaves and servants crawled up on their knees, and bowed before him. They bowed so low that their foreheads knocked the floor. All of them had headaches, and big bruises on their foreheads, from bowing down and knocking their heads so much!

When the slaves and servants had bowed and knocked their heads many times, the sultan would go to his balcony and sit on a great throne, facing the east. Then he would say: "Sun, you may rise, and feast your shining eye upon my greatness. But, though you are big and bright, and wonderful to see, you are not one thousandth part as wonderful as I!"

Well, of course the sun would rise, but only because it was the right time for it!

One morning, the sultan slept late. His slaves and servants were afraid to wake him, because he would be angry at that.

So, that day, the sun rose without the sultan's permission! Naturally, the sun didn't need anyone's permission to rise. But the vain, silly sultan thought it did!

When the sultan woke, and saw what the sun had done, he was so angry he almost exploded. "How does the sun dare to rise, before I tell it to?" he shouted. The slaves and servants trembled with fear, and knocked their heads against the floor harder than ever. But, for once, the sultan didn't punish them.

He jumped out of bed and rushed to the balcony in his wonderful nightshirt, of many fine colours. "Go back!" he screamed at the sun. "Go back and wait till I call you!"

The sun stayed where it was.

"Yeeeeeek!" cried the sultan, in such a rage as he'd never been in before. "If you don't go back at once, I shall put you in a dungeon and never let you out again!"

Silly man! Of course the sun stayed right where it was.

He reached out to grasp the disobedient sun and pull it down. He couldn't reach it. He climbed on the balcony railing, and stretched out again. Still he couldn't touch the sun. This made him angrier than ever, and he jumped up and down in fury. He leaped about so much, he jumped right off the balcony!

Down he fell, with a tremendous crash, and was completely squashed.

Everyone cheered, because they were free of that wicked sultan.

Soon they had a new sultan, but he was a good, kind man. He set the slaves and prisoners free, and the bright sun shone down on a very happy land.

The Greatest Thing in All Nepal

In Asia, in a country named Nepal, is a jungle named the Terai. In it lived a proud tiger, who believed he was the greatest thing in all Nepal. So one day, he set out to tell everyone.

He left the jungle and climbed over a great range of mountains called the Lesser Himalayas. "Fancy calling them *lesser*," thought the tiger, who had quite a struggle to cross them. At last he came to a great valley, full of farms.

"I am the greatest thing in all Nepal!" he roared. No one argued. Man, bird and beast, all ran from the proud tiger's roar.

Farther up the valley, in the city of Katmandu, he roared out his news again. As before, everyone ran off. Except for one brave boy.

"You're *not* the greatest thing in all Nepal," he said. "Mount Everest is greater than you. It's the biggest mountain in the world!"

"We'll see about that!" growled the tiger. "I shall climb Mount Everest, and prove that *I* am the greatest. Off he went. He had thought the Lesser Himalayas were big enough, but when he came to the Greater Himalayas, he soon knew why one was called Lesser and the other Greater!

He came to Mount Everest. Up it he went, up and up, till he was higher than a tiger had ever been before. He climbed until he could not climb another inch. Still Mount Everest rose into the clouds high above him.

The tiger gave up.

"All right, I admit it. Mount Everest is the greatest thing in all Nepal," he growled. And then he roared: "But I'm still the greatest tiger!" No one argued. So the greatest *tiger* in all Nepal turned and went home.

THE NETHERLANDS

Stop That Cheese!

In the Netherlands, in the country near Edam, they make round cheeses covered with red wax.

One day a farmer asked a bargeman to help him to take some cheeses to town. They piled the cheeses on the barge, and set off. But on the way they stopped for lunch. "Let's have some cheese," said the farmer, reaching out for one. But the cheese he reached for didn't want to be eaten. He wanted to stay just as he was, wrapped up in his bright red coat. So he jumped off the barge, on to the bank, and rolled away just as fast as he could!

"Hey! Stop that cheese!" cried the farmer, and ran after it. "Yes, stop!" bellowed the bargeman, running after the farmer. And behind both of them came the bargeman's dog, howling and barking and enjoying himself no end!

But the cheese rolled on . . . into a field where some gardeners were picking tulips. "A runaway cheese!" shrieked a woman. She dropped her flowers and ran after it.

"Mind my tulips!" wailed the tulip grower, and he dashed after her. Behind him came all the other gardeners, the farmer and the bargeman. And behind them all came the dog, howling and barking.

The cheese rolled on, as fast as a cheese can roll, into the town. He rolled past a horse, who reared up and nearly tipped his cart. "Hey! Mind my potatoes!" screamed the carter. And began chasing the cheese, potato cart and all. Behind came the woman, the tulip grower, the gardeners, the farmer, the bargeman, and last of all the dog.

The cheese was very tired. He bounced against a pair of feet and there he came to rest. He didn't have a bounce left in him! Lucky cheese! The feet belonged to a girl named Wilna who picked him up. She looked at the carter, the woman, the tulip grower, the gardeners, the farmer, the bargeman and the dog. They were all making a great noise.

"Quiet, you noisy lot!" cried Wilna. "You ought to be ashamed, chasing a poor cheese like that. Why, he's quite frightened!"

Well, that made the carter, the woman, the tulip grower, the gardeners, the farmer and the bargeman feel a bit ashamed of themselves. So they all stopped making a noise—even the dog—and went away.

Then Wilna took the cheese home, and put him where he could look out the window. So if you're ever in Edam, and see a cheeky cheese looking at you, well, you know all about *him*!

Birds of the Gods

The most beautiful birds in all the world live on the island of New Guinea. Some people call them birds of paradise. The people of the island call them the birds of the gods.

At one time hunters used to come to the island to catch the birds and steal their fine feathers, for silly people to wear in their hats.

But the gods of New Guinea liked to look down from the hills and watch their beautiful birds playing and flying in the forests. The hunters made them very angry.

So the next time a hunter went into the forest—whump! Down came a big net and caught him!

"Scrumble-dee-bee, scrumble-dee-boo,

A plague of feathers on the likes of you!" roared a great voice. Then the net vanished.

The hunter ran clear out of the forest and right down to the beach. There he met some other hunters, who could hardly believe their eyes—for he was covered all over with feathers! They tried to pull them off, only to find that they were sticky-sneezy feathers! They stuck to *all* the hunters.

What a mess they all got into—tugging and pulling and getting more and more stuck with feathers, and all the time sneezing and *sneezing!* At last they could tug and pull no more, and so they all climbed into their boat and sailed and sneezed away, and never came back again.

The Clever Kiwi

Many, many centuries ago, nobody lived on the islands of New Zealand. Then the Maori people came from Polynesia and made their homes on North Island.

They were a great sea-faring people, who travelled hundreds of miles across the wide Pacific Ocean in outrigger canoes. Whole families went in the canoes—fathers, mothers, children, babies and all.

When the Maoris first reached North Island, they were very hungry. So they all went hunting. One of them found a kiwi bird. It was such a strange creature, the Maori wasn't sure he could eat it.

"Are you a bird?" he asked it. "If you are, where are your wings? I don't think I can eat a bird who hasn't any wings."

Now it so happens that kiwis *do* have wings, even if they can't fly with them. Because they are only two inches long. The kiwis stick their heads under their wings when they go to sleep. When they're awake and walking about, their wings don't show.

But this kiwi was no fool. He didn't want to be eaten, so he said: "Wings? Of course I haven't got any wings. So you can't eat me, can you? But if you like, I'll show you some food." He toddled off on his little short legs, and the man followed him.

Soon they came to some bushes loaded with berries. The man began to pick them. While he was busy, the kiwi scuttled off, and didn't stop till he was hidden far away in the deep forest. He didn't want the Maoris to discover he had wings after all!

Today, everyone loves the funny kiwi birds, and no one hunts them. But the kiwis are taking no chances of being caught. They still hide in the deep forests.

NICARAGUA

Going to Chinandega

Isabella and Luciano lived on a farm in the centre of Nicaragua, which is in the centre of Central America.

One day their father said: "I am buying some sheep for the farm, some very special sheep. I am going all the way to the city of Chinandega to buy them!"

"Please let us come," begged Luciano. "I could help you with the sheep."

"So could I," said Isabella. "Besides, we've never seen Chinandega."

"Very well," said their father. "And there's something else at Chinandega that you've never seen before. But I won't tell you what it is. It will be a surprise."

So off they went. They rode in their ox cart, which had two big, solid wooden wheels to run on, and two big, solid oxen to pull it. The journey to Chinandega is a long one, and it took them several days. They travelled through fields and forests and over many rivers. Luciano asked his father where all the rivers went to.

"Most of them run into Lake Nicaragua," said his father. "In fact, forty-five rivers run into it—and it's so big, you can't see one side from the other."

The next day, they travelled through coffee plantations, which stretched all the way to the horizon. The day after that, they passed mile after mile of cotton fields. The cotton was ready for picking, and it hung on the bushes like balls of white wool. And the day after *that,* they saw *another* new thing— a great line of blue stretching right across the edge of the world. "What is it?" they asked.

"Water," said their father.

"Lake Nicaragua!" cried Isabella.

"No, no," laughed their father. "That's the surprise I promised you. It's the Pacific Ocean.

They drove to the shore. The sea made them feel small. Why, just one of its waves was taller than Isabella and Luciano together!

Then they went into Chinandega and bought six sheep, the finest sheep they had ever seen. Their wool was thick and springy, and they had funny black faces.

Chinandega was a fine city, but they were glad to leave it next day, for it meant they were going home again. Luciano walked behind the cart and drove the sheep along.

At last they reached their home in the hills, and put the sheep in a fine green pasture. Isabella and Luciano took care of them. And later, when some lovely lambs were born, they took care of them, too.

The Lost Brother

In the north of Nigeria is the city of Kano. It is the meeting place of the great camel caravans, on their long travels across Africa.

In that city two brothers, Hassan and Ali, were born and grew up. They played together under its palm trees and in the shade of its mud walls. But their favourite place was the camping spot of the caravans. To them these caravans, with their long-legged, bad-tempered camels loaded with mysterious goods were the most wonderful things in the world. They wanted to go with them.

One day, they did. When they were almost grown, they joined a caravan on its way to fabled lands.

But, on their very first trip, the fierce, dry Harmattan wind swept down on them. It filled the air with dust, till a rider couldn't see his camel's head. The caravan stopped and huddled together. But the wind was cruel. It swept away a camel, and with it went young Ali.

They searched and searched, but found no sign of Ali. Hassan was broken hearted, and grieved for his brother.

Years later, Hassan was still travelling with the long caravans, back and forth across the continent. One day, he brought his caravan into Kano, the city of his birth. There he met another caravan. Hassan raised his hand to its leader: "Greetings, brother traveller."

The stranger also raised his hand. He too said: "Greetings . . ." and then he shouted: "*Brother*!" It was Ali! Both young men leapt from their camels, and raced to embrace one another.

Then Ali told his tale—of how, lost in the storm, he was found by another caravan. It took him north, to the great Sahara desert. And only now, after years of wandering, had he found his way home to Kano.

From then on the two brothers spent their lives travelling to distant places, and were never more parted.

NORWAY

Waterlogged!

When Fatima and Shamsuzzakir went to Norway on their magic carpet, they met a fishing fleet.

"Let's do some fishing ourselves," said Shamsuzzakir, who liked fishing a lot.

So Fatima made the carpet hover over the waves while he fished. What a sight they made, sitting above the water on their bright carpet!

Then Shamsuzzakir pulled up a fish. It flapped and splashed, and the carpet wriggled, for it didn't like having a wet fish sitting on it. Disaster! The carpet bumped into a wave and they began to sink!

"Help!" they cried, for the carpet was too wet to fly.

Some fishermen threw out a net and drew them safely on board. They gave the children dry clothes and hung the carpet on the mast to dry.

Fatima and Shamsuzzakir thanked the fishermen for saving them. They brushed down the carpet to clean away the fish scales and salt. And they promised never to fish from the magic carpet again.

The Tidal Wave

There are thousands of Pacific Islands, scattered like confetti over the wide ocean. The *Laughing Susan* was a trading ship. She sailed about the islands, carrying cargo and news.

One day, when sailing to a tiny island, she met all the islanders in their canoes. They were paddling as fast as they could away from the island.

The skipper of the *Laughing Susan* hailed the canoes: "Ahoy! What's wrong?"

Up stood the island chief, shouting in great excitement. "We don't know exactly, but something is, because when we woke this morning, we were all very frightened. So we came away!"

The skipper was a brave man who wasn't easily scared. He went to the island, to see what was the matter. But the frightened islanders paddled away quickly, in the other direction.

When the skipper went ashore, the island looked quite peaceful. He could see nothing wrong. But it *did* feel wrong. And like the islanders, even the brave captain was frightened. So he sailed after the canoes, caught them up, and took everyone on board. Then he sailed away as fast as the *Laughing Susan* could go.

Suddenly, a huge wave, far higher than the top of the *Laughing Susan's* mast, was racing at them! It was a tidal wave!

It struck the *Laughing Susan*, lashing and roaring and trying to sink her. But she climbed the steep wave, up and up, till her bows pointed straight at the sky. Then she was over the crest, and sliding down the back of the wave. Soon the wave was far away, leaving them unhurt and safe.

They sailed back to the island. The wave had run right over it, sweeping it clean of every house and tree. "We were right to be frightened," said the islanders. But it's a mystery *how* they were frightened, for no one knew the tidal wave was coming.

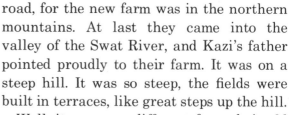

PAKISTAN

The Country in Two Parts

Kazi lived in East Pakistan, on a farm where they grew rice. It was a very wet place, for it was in the delta of the Ganges River, where the river slows down and spreads out as it comes close to the sea. It was so wet, they built their bamboo house on stilts, to keep the water out when there were floods.

Kazi's parents wanted to live in a drier part, so his father set out to look for one. At last he sent a letter telling Kazi and his mother to come to West Pakistan.

Now, Pakistan is in two parts, one to the east of India, and one to the west. And the best way to travel from East Pakistan to West Pakistan is by aeroplane. So Kazi and his mother rode on an aeroplane for the first time. His Father met them at the airport and then they travelled a long way by road, for the new farm was in the northern mountains. At last they came into the valley of the Swat River, and Kazi's father pointed proudly to their farm. It was on a steep hill. It was so steep, the fields were built in terraces, like great steps up the hill.

Well, it was very different from their old farm! It certainly wasn't wet on the hill, and their house was built of stone and stood on the ground, not on stilts. And they didn't grow rice, they grew wheat. But they all liked it very much, and were happy there.

The Shy Tapir

Right in the deepest, wildest part of a jungle in Panama, there lived a tapir. She was a strange animal, who looked a bit like a horse and a bit like a rhinoceros. She was about six feet long and she had a little trunk. It was like an elephant's trunk, but very short.

She was very shy, and liked to be on her own. So she hid away quietly in the deep jungle, and never made a sound. She just wandered about, eating leaves and fruit. Every once in a while she went to a salt lick. She was always afraid to go there, because there were usually other animals about. But like all the other animals, she needed salt to stay healthy.

One day, all afraid and nervous, she crept towards the salt lick. Every few steps, she stopped and looked and listened, but she saw no one and heard nothing. So she stepped out of the trees and began snuffling at the salt in the earth.

But it happened that there *was* one other animal there. Up in a tree slept a lonely monkey. He had lost the rest of his tribe, and had been wandering for days, all by himself.

The sound of the tapir snuffling at the salt lick woke him up. He had never seen such a strange animal before, but she seemed a nice, pleasant animal. He thought he'd like to make friends with her, so he jumped down and landed on her back.

Wow! The tapir was so surprised, she nearly fell down! Then she dashed away, as fast as her little short legs could go. She ran so fast, the monkey was afraid to jump off. He clung on to her back.

Kersplollop! The tapir threw herself into a deep pond. The monkey was beginning to feel less frightened now. He quite liked swimming, especially if someone else was doing all the work. The tapir swam for a long time, and when she got tired the monkey jumped off and climbed up a tree.

He picked some fruit and threw it down to the tapir. At first she hid in a bush. But finally she crept out and ate a piece. Then she ate some more, and so did the monkey.

Now the tapir is not so shy as she used to be. She's made friends with the monkey. He picks fruit from the trees for her. And she takes him swimming every day.

PARAGUAY

The Football Armadillo

Arturo was an armadillo. He lived in the Chaco of Paraguay, which is in the middle of South America. He was covered with armour—on his back, his legs, his tail and the top of his head. The armour on his back and his tail was jointed, so it would bend. In fact, it would bend so well, that he could roll himself up into a ball. That way, his armour covered him all over.

Arturo lived in a burrow. Usually he came out only at night, to look for food. But one day he heard heavy footsteps tramping back and forth over his head. He peeped out, and saw several men. They were carrying lots of wood and stone and tools. Arturo sat and watched them for hours. They built a house!

It was a big house, and when it was finished the men moved in with their families. Then they dug up and planted some fields. But most of the ground they left for grass. They brought in hundreds of cattle to eat it. Arturo was right in the middle of a new cattle ranch!

Arturo liked that very much. There were so many strange new things, he never grew tired of watching. No one ever noticed him there, for he sat very still in his burrow.

The thing he liked best was watching the men and boys play football in the evenings. He became a great football fan, and would cheer to himself when anyone scored.

Then, one day, the football got away from a boy and ran right up to Arturo. He was so interested, he forgot all about hiding. He ran out of his burrow and gave the football a kick. "This is fun!" he thought. But, oh dear! Arturo had long, sharp claws, and when he kicked the ball, he tore a big hole in it. . . . *Hiss*. All the air came out of it.

The boy came running up, so Arturo dashed back into his burrow. When he looked out, the boy was holding the torn football and crying. "It's ruined. Now we can't play football any more," he said.

"It's all my fault," Arturo said to himself. "I wish I could do something to make up for it." Then he had a wonderful idea. He curled himself up into a ball, and rolled out of his burrow, right to the boy's feet.

"Look!" shouted the boy. "Here's an armadillo who wants to play football!"

He was right. Arturo *did* want to play football. In fact, he wanted to *be* a football.

The boy gave Arturo a push with his foot, and Arturo rolled across the grass. Since everyone played with bare feet, and he had his armour plating on, it didn't hurt him a bit! Soon everyone was playing football with Arturo and having a marvellous time.

And Arturo had the best time of all.

Why Hummingbirds Hum

Once upon a time all the birds in the world gathered in Peru in South America to have a singing contest. All the animals came too, to be the judges. Every bird had to sing his own song. The very air tingled with music,

When every bird had sung his song, they asked the judges to say which song was best. But they couldn't decide, because there were so many songs they liked. So, instead, they chose all the best singers—all 319 of them!

Then the 319 best singers gave a concert, and what a concert! Nothing like it will ever be heard again, for the 319 birds sang and trilled and whistled and warbled so long and so loud, they completely lost their voices. They would never sing again! They could only twitter and squeak.

They were so sad, all 319 just sat down and cried. And so did all the other birds, and the animals too.

But the peacock thought of a way to cheer them up. "I'll give one of you some of my beautiful blue colour," he said.

"What a good idea!" everyone agreed. So they all gave something of themselves. They gave the sad birds beauty and speed and strength and brightness and happiness. They turned those sad birds into the most wonderful little birds in the world.

The 319 birds leapt up in the air and flew for pure thankfulness. They swooped and hovered and darted forwards and backwards. Their wings moved so fast, they couldn't be seen—but they could be heard! Every tiny wing hummed as it moved, making a sound of happiness. The 319 birds were singing with their wings.

The concert ended then, but the wings of those birds are still humming. That's why we call them hummingbirds.

The Gigantic Yam

In a town in the Philippine Islands grew the biggest yam in the world. It was in Mrs Mapa's garden, and its huge vine covered her house. Everyone came to look at the vine, and to guess how big the root had grown.

One day Mrs Mapa said to her friends: "Today I shall dig up the yam. Tonight we'll we'll have fried yam, boiled yam, mashed yam, spiced yam, pickled yam, cold yam and hot yam to eat."

Her friends licked their lips, and Mrs Mapa began to dig. She dug for an hour, and still she hadn't uncovered the whole root.

When her hungry friends returned again that evening, they found a great pit in the ground. Down at the bottom were Mrs Mapa and the biggest yam root ever seen! They threw down a rope, and pulled out Mrs Mapa. Then they put the ropes round the great yam root. They pulled and hauled and heaved and tugged till finally, out came the yam. It was half as big as the house!

They were all very hungry after their hard work, so they cut a big slice from the yam. They cooked it seven different ways and ate it. Every day they came back and had another slice. It took them four months to eat that yam!

Avalanche!

It was wintertime when Fatima and Shamsuzzakir visited Poland on their magic carpet. Snow covered the land and blew through the air. It was very cold, so they wore long coats and big boots and warm hats and mittens.

They flew over snowy plains and frozen rivers, till they came to the mountains. There they saw a tiny village. A crowd of people stood in the street. They were all looking up the mountain and pointing.

Shamsuzzakir steered the magic carpet down, and they landed in the street.

All the people ran up to the magic carpet. "Have you come to help us?" they asked.

"What's wrong?" asked Shamsuzzakir.

The people pointed up the mountain. "Look at all the snow hanging over us," they said. "There have been big snowstorms for a month. Now the snow is so thick and heavy, we're afraid it will fall down the mountain. It will make an avalanche and bury our village!"

Fatima and Shamsuzzakir looked up the mountain. It was very frightening, for there *was* a great deal of snow up there. *And* it looked all ready to fall down.

"Why don't you run away down the mountain, where the snow can't reach you?" they asked.

"We would if we could," said the people. "But the road is covered with snow, so deep it's right over your head. We can't get through. The only way out of here is by helicopter. But we don't have a helicopter."

"Why, *we* can fly you out," said Fatima.

Some of the people were frightened of flying on the magic carpet. But they were more afraid of the avalanche! Everyone— girls and boys, mothers and fathers, grand-mothers and grandfathers—hopped on to the carpet.

"Let's go!" shouted Shamsuzzakir. But the carpet couldn't fly! The load of people was too heavy. It slid slowly over the snow.

"Hurry, hurry!" called the people. "The avalanche has started!"

A great frozen river of snow was pouring down the mountain, straight for them!

"Oh, what shall we do?" squeaked Fatima.

"Hang on tight!" cried her brother. He steered the carpet to point it down the mountain. It slid, faster and faster over the snow, like a toboggan. Soon it was zooming down, with the avalanche chasing behind!

"Faster, faster!" cried the people. "The snow is catching us!"

The carpet hit a bump and bounded into the air. At last it was flying. It staggered and wobbled under its heavy load, but it flew! And it left the avalanche far behind, at the bottom of the mountain.

Ernesto the Sailor

Ernesto lived in Portugal, which is a small country on the western edge of Europe. One day he set out to see the world.

At that time—five hundred years ago—there were no trains, cars or aeroplanes. People didn't even know how big the world was.

So when Ernesto said he was going to see the world, he really meant a very small part of it. He walked hundreds of miles, through mountains and valleys, until at last he came to the city of Lisbon, which is by the sea.

Lisbon was a fine place, the finest Ernesto had ever seen. But, best of all, he liked the ships in the harbour. He had never been on a ship. He wanted to try a bit of sailing, but no one would give him a ride.

"These are working boats," the sailors said. "We don't give pleasure trips. Go away!"

But Ernesto hid away in the deep hold of a big ship and waited for it to sail. While he waited, he fell asleep. When he woke,

they were far out to sea. And he didn't like it at all! The ship tossed and slid about on the waves and made his stomach feel very bad indeed. He crawled up to the deck. "Take me back. I'm so sick!" he said to a man.

That man was the captain. He roared with laughter. "A seasick stowaway! And he wants us to turn back! Ho, not likely, my boy! We're off to explore the coast of Africa!"

Ernesto was on a ship that planned to sail farther than any Portuguese ship had sailed before. It wasn't going home for months!

"Since you're here," the captain told him, "you'd better do some work, or you won't be fed!" So Ernesto became a sailor.

He soon stopped feeling seasick, and enjoyed being a sailor. The ship sailed far, far into unknown waters. He saw many strange lands and people. Months later, the ship returned to Lisbon. Then the captain said to Ernest: "*Now* you can leave the ship—if you wish."

But Ernesto stayed with the ship and went on many voyages. In fact he sailed the sea for all his long life, and he learned that the world was much, much bigger than he had ever dreamed.

RHODESIA

The Water God and the Turaco

The great Zambezi River, on its way across Africa, passes through Rhodesia. And there it hurls itself over a cliff to make the wonderful, roaring Victoria Falls. Some of the great noise is made by the water against the rocks. And some of it is the water god laughing.

Did you know there's a water god in every waterfall? If you watch closely, you will see one. When you first look at a waterfall, you see only water pouring down. But keep on staring, and you'll see an upward movement in the water. That's the water god dancing!

Once the god in Victoria Falls was un-happy. His animal friends asked him what

The Water Wheel

On a farm in Rumania there were a horse, a water wheel and a naughty boy. Every day the boy took the horse from its stable and harnessed it to the water wheel. Then he sat on the wheel, whacked the horse with a stick, and shouted at it. The horse walked round and round, turning the wheel. That turned other wheels. The final wheel dipped deep below the ground, scooped up water, and poured it into a trough. The water ran across the farmyard and into the fields, where the thirsty cabbages drank it.

All day long the patient horse trudged round and round, lifting water from the earth. And all day long the boy sat on the wheel and whacked him with a stick.

One day the horse said to the boy: "Please stop hitting me with that stick."

But the boy whacked even harder! "You never go fast enough. Go faster!" he shouted.

At that the patient horse finally lost his patience. "Right you are, my lad!"

He broke into a trot, and then a canter.

Water spurted from the wheel. The boy got quite dizzy. "That's fast enough!" he cried. "Slow down!" The horse ignored him. Faster again he went, till he was galloping like a race horse. The water flooded out. It turned the farmyard into a mud patch.

Finally the wheel went so fast—the boy was flung clear off it. He landed *squelch*—flat on his face in the mud! Then the horse stopped galloping and laughed.

After that the boy became very good, and he never hit his horse again.

was wrong. "My feelings are hurt," he said. "Everyone comes to see me. Everyone except the turaco bird. He never comes."

At once the animals hurried into the forest and found a beautiful turaco.

"I'd gladly come and see him," said the turaco, "but it's all that water spraying about. It takes the colour out of my wings!"

But the other animals dragged him, complaining bitterly, back to the falls. They told the water god what was wrong. A great splash of water came from the falls and showered all over the turaco.

The turaco shrieked, "Oh, no! My beautiful green feathers will fade!"

"That was magic water," said the god. "Your colour will never run again!"

And it didn't. Now the turaco often goes to Victoria Falls to see the great sight and have a chat with his friend the water god.

The Captured Markhor

In the Turkestan area of Russia live the curly-horned markhor goats. One day a hunter climbed a mountain to catch one of them. The markhors saw him coming, and laughed proudly. "He'll never catch us," they said. "We can climb faster and higher and better than a man."

All day long the man chased the markhors. "Silly man," they laughed. "We're not afraid of you."

Then the man slipped, and rolled down the mountain. He landed at the bottom of a cliff, and he didn't move.

"He's hurt," said Ivan markhor.

"Too bad. It's his own fault for trying to catch us," said the others.

But Ivan felt sorry for the man. He went to the top of the cliff. "Throw me your rope and I'll pull you up," he called.

The man threw his rope. Ivan caught it round his curly horns, and in his strong teeth. He pulled the man up the cliff.

"Thank you," said the man. "Please help me home, for my leg hurts and I can't walk."

All the other markhors cried out. "Don't go, Ivan! It's a trap to catch you!"

But Ivan let the man climb on his back, and carried him down the mountain. The other markhors followed, a long way behind.

Ivan carried the man right into his village. Crowds of people ran from the houses. They caught Ivan and put him in a stable.

"Poor Ivan!" sighed his friends. "We'll never see him again." They were very sad.

Next morning they heard a great noise from the village. There was cheering, and laughter, and loud music.

The markhors groaned. "That noise means the people are having a celebration. Probably a feast – a feast of markhor! Poor old Ivan!"

They hid in the trees and peered out at the village, very afraid. Then they saw Ivan.

The villagers were having a festival, and Ivan was the guest of honour! His hair was brushed and gleaming, and tied with bright ribbons. Garlands of pretty flowers circled his horns. Children danced round him, and fed him cakes and biscuits and jelly and apples.

When the party was over, Ivan left the village, quite unhurt. He met his friends, the other markhors. "That was quite a festival," he said. "My people friends have asked me to come back next year, to be the guest of honour again."

The other markhors were quite jealous of Ivan. So next year, when festival time came round, they all went to the village. And they all had a marvellous time.

RWANDA

The Sunbird

In Rwanda, which is a small country in the middle of Africa, lived a mother and her baby. Every day she worked in her fields, hoeing and weeding her maize and sweet potatoes. Sometimes she carried her baby in a sling on her back as she worked. Sometimes she laid him in the shade of a bush.

In the evening she went back to her house and cooked food. She always ate up all her own food, for she worked hard and she was hungry. But the baby never ate anything. He was never hungry. And yet he grew fatter every day!

The mother wondered if someone else was feeding him. She wondered who. She wondered why. So, one morning, she laid him under a bush by the field, as she always did. But she didn't go to the field. She hid behind the bush.

After a while the baby woke up and cried. Down flew a bright sunbird and popped a juicy ripe berry in his mouth. The baby ate the berry, while the sunbird fanned him with her wing. She even whistled a pretty tune.

The mother jumped from behind the bush.

"Why are you feeding my baby?" she asked.

"Oh, oh, oh," cried the sunbird, fluttering and hopping about in surprise. "My nest fell out of the tree, and all my eggs got broken, and now I have no babies of my own to feed. So I thought I'd feed this one. I hope you don't mind."

The mother laughed and laughed. She patted the sunbird and said: "I don't mind at all."

Soon they were good friends. Every day after that, the mother worked in her fields and the sunbird looked after her baby.

Jasper and the Butterfly

Jasper was a friendly jaguar who lived in a swampy jungle in Salvador. He was like a great big cat, even if he was bigger than the tallest man. He had a long tail and soft fur with lovely yellow and black spots.

One hot day he was lying in the shade of a tree, when a butterfly came fluttering along. She thought the jaguar's spots were flowers, so she landed on the jaguar's back.

Wasn't she surprised when the flowers turned out to be the spots on Jasper's fur!

"Ooo!" she gasped. She was so scared, she couldn't move.

Jasper lifted up his long tail. The butterfly quaked with fear. "Oh dear," she cried, "he'll squash me flat—I know he will!"

"Don't be so silly," said the jaguar, "why on earth would I do a thing like that? I don't want to hurt you. I'm Jasper the friendly jaguar. Come and play some games!"

Well, the butterfly was still scared, but she didn't want to annoy Jasper—no matter how friendly he said he was. So she played with him. They had running-flying races, and they played hide and seek, and then they played hopscotch. (The butterfly always won at hopscotch, but Jasper didn't mind.)

Soon Jasper and the little butterfly became very good friends and the butterfly wasn't scared any more. After that they played together every day.

SAN MARINO

The Ugly Prince

In the foothills of the Apennine Mountains is tiny San Marino, the oldest country in Europe. Once, long ago, an ugly prince lived there. He was so ugly, babies cried, dogs howled, and birds flew away when they saw him. So the poor prince hid his face by wearing a velvet bag over his head.

When the prince grew up, his father sent word all over Europe, in the hope of finding a princess for his son to marry. But they had all heard of the ugly prince. Not even the plainest princess wanted to marry him. The people of San Marino were very sad for the prince. They wept and sobbed and cried all day, and they sniffled and wailed and blubbered all night.

There wasn't a dry eye in the whole of San Marino. Streams of tears ran down the streets and made a deep sad pool at the bottom of the hill. The birds stopped singing, the flowers drooped, and the sun hid behind a cloud.

Even the prince, who was used to unhappiness, sat in his garden and cried. And the velvet bag over his head became so wet with tears, he pulled it off.

A breeze blew over the wall and dried his face. It also brought a tiny white handkerchief and blew it against the prince's ugly face. The handkerchief was wet with tears, and it was embroidered with a name—*Ailsa*.

The prince knew Ailsa was the baker's daughter. He took the handkerchief to her house. When he knocked she came to the door, her pretty face all wet from crying.

"I found your handkerchief," said the prince, and he gave it to her.

"Thank you," said Ailsa. "Who are you?"

"Why, I'm the ugly prince, of course," he said. "Everyone knows me, because I wear this bag over my head."

"But there's no bag on your head," Ailsa replied. "And besides, you're not ugly."

The prince put his hand to his head. The bag wasn't there—he'd forgotten to put it on again! He rushed into the baker's house and looked in a mirror. *What* a surprise! He wasn't ugly any more. In fact, he was quite handsome. He ran home to tell his parents. Ailsa ran to tell everyone else. Soon the whole town was laughing for joy. The birds sang, the flowers raised their heads, the sun came out, and the sad pool of tears dried up.

"*Now* we'll find you a fine princess to marry," said the prince's father happily.

But the prince didn't want to marry any fine princess. He wanted Ailsa. "It was the tears from her handkerchief that wiped away my ugliness," he said.

So Ailsa and the prince were married. And neither of them ever cried again.

On the Way to Mecca

Saudi Arabia is a big country, taking up most of the Arabian peninsula. Its most famous place is Mecca, the holy city of the Moslem religion. Moslems travel from all over the world to visit its great mosques and shrines.

Many hundreds of miles from Mecca, deep in the desert, lived an oryx named Hassan. He looked like any other oryx—mostly white, with black legs, and black patches on his face, and two long, fine horns. But Hassan was different. He was a *Moslem* oryx, and he was travelling to Mecca. He was taking a long time to get there, for he had to walk. But every day he travelled a few miles more, and he was quite happy. "Some day I will reach the great and beautiful city," he told himself.

But one day, as Hassan walked along, a man jumped from behind a rock. He threw a lassoo and caught Hassan by the horns!

"Help! Help!" cried poor Hassan. He struggled and pulled, but the man held the rope tight.

"It's all right. Don't upset yourself," said the man. "I've only caught you so I can take you to a nice, safe zoo. There aren't very many oryx left in the desert. If I don't save some of you, soon you'll all be dead and gone."

Hassan thought it was very kind of the man to want to save him. But he didn't want to go to a zoo. So he said: "I'm sorry, but I'm on my way to Mecca."

Now, that surprised the man very much, for he had never heard of such a thing. He was so surprised, he dropped the rope!

Quick as a flash, Hassan pulled his horns free from the rope. Then he dashed away, as fast as his little black legs could go. Soon he was safely out of sight, over a hill.

So if you ever go on a trip to Mecca, look out for Hassan. When last heard of, he still had many long miles to go. But he's sure to get there some day.

SCOTLAND

Emma's Paisley Shawl

Emma went to visit her grandmother in Paisley. The town is famous for weaving cloth with a special design in many colours. The beautiful design is called Paisley, too.

Emma's grandmother gave her a silk Paisley shawl. Emma loved it. It was so beautiful, she took it to show to all her friends.

First, she went to a pasture on a farm. She stood on the gate and waved her shawl to the lambs. They came running to look at it. All of them touched their noses against it, to feel how silky it was. "I wish I had a shawl as fine as that to wear," said one of them.

"But you're already wearing a fine wool coat," said Emma. "You're very lucky, because you don't have to dress and undress every day, but I do."

The lambs thought about it, and decided that Emma was right. They *were* lucky! But they still liked her Paisley shawl.

Soon, the news of Emma's Paisley shawl had spread all over the moor. Hedgehogs, shrews, moles, voles, rabbits, mice, weasels, stoats and foxes all came to admire it. Even a shy wild cat peeped over a rock to see it.

When everyone had looked at the shawl, Emma said goodbye and went on to the wood. There she met the deer, her very special friends. Mrs Deer liked the shawl very much, so Emma let her wear it over her back for a while. "Now I have something to show you," said Mrs Deer. She led Emma through the wood, and Mr Deer came along behind. They went to a grassy clearing and there, sleeping in the sun, was a tiny fawn.

"He's lovely," said Emma. "Why, he's as beautiful as my Paisley shawl!"

The fawn went back to sleep. Emma wrapped herself in her shawl and lay down beside him. She had come a long way and was very tired, so soon she was fast asleep. Mr and Mrs Deer kept watch over her and the fawn.

When the fawn woke up, Emma was still asleep. "She must be very tired," said Mrs Deer.

It's getting late. We'd best take her home," said Mr Deer. So they picked up the shawl in their mouths, with sleeping Emma still wrapped up in it. They carried her all the way home, with the fawn tagging along behind.

Emma's grandmother saw them coming. She brought the deer some salt, for they like salt as much as children like sweets.

Emma woke up, and said goodbye to her friends. Then her grandmother took her in and put her to bed, for Emma was quite a little girl. Soon she was asleep again, with her beautiful Paisley shawl spread over her.

The Hungry Lion

In the hot, dry Ferlo desert of Senegal lived a boy who kept a herd of goats. They travelled all over the desert looking for grass and water. Now, also in the desert lived a big lion. His home was on a small, rocky hill. But when he was hungry he too would search the desert for food.

One day he set out to find himself a goat. But the boy had led his herd in a great circle so, no sooner had the lion left his home, when the boy and his goats moved in!

Well, of course the lion could not find the goats. But when he came back, still hungry, he saw them on his hill. "Well, how very thoughtful of them," he said. "They've brought themselves straight to my larder!" He bounded up the hill.

"Whack!" a pebble shot out and hit him. The lion yelped and ran back. The boy was hurling pebbles from his slingshot!

The lion stayed out of range, but he wouldn't go away. If he couldn't get up the hill then the goats weren't going to get down it! Days passed. Lion, boy and goats all grew faint with hunger.

SIERRA LEONE

The Monkey Explorer

Sierra Leone is a hot country, on the West Africa coast. Green Colobus monkeys live there, high in the trees. Did you ever hear of a green monkey before? They're really rust red, with a green tint.

Long ago, there was a Green Colobus monkey baby named Boo. At a very early age, he became an explorer. He soon knew every leaf and branch, vine and flower for miles around his home tree. Then he discovered the empty spaces.

The empty spaces in the deep Sierra Leone forests are on the ground. You see, the trees grow quite wide apart at the bottom. At the top they spread out their branches. They mix and tangle themselves so closely, that no sunlight gets through to the ground. Nothing grows there.

Well, when Boo saw that, he just had to have a closer look. He slithered down a tree trunk, to the ground. But there was nothing to see, except bare red earth. It was very gloomy, and very lonely. Boo wanted to go home again. But he couldn't get back up the tree! "Boo-hoo!" cried Boo. "Boo-hoo!"

What a tremendous noise he made! The sound bounced about the tree trunks, and filled the tree tops. "Stop that awful row," cried all the monkeys.

Finally Boo's mother climbed down and took him back home. But she had to use both hands for climbing up, so she held Boo in her mouth. And until Boo was much older, she carried him in her mouth wherever they went.

At first, all the other Green Colobus monkey mothers thought Boo and his mother looked very funny, going around like that. Then they tried it, and found it rather handy. Soon they were *all* carrying their babies about in their mouths.

Well, that was a long time ago. But Green Colobus monkey mothers still carry their babies about in their mouths.

"Give me just one little goat," begged the lion, with his belly rumbling emptily.

"You shan't have a single hair from a single goat of mine!" shouted the boy.

Then up flew Fatima and Shamsuzzakir on the magic carpet. No one knows how they knew they were needed, but there they were!

First they dropped some bales of hay for the goats and a bag of food for the boy. They threw the lion a big piece of meat and then, while he was eating it, scooped him up—meat and all—and carried him off out of the desert to where there were lots of wild animals, and no boys with slingshots!

SINGAPORE

Lim Lin's Pineapples

Lim Lin lived on a pineapple farm on Singapore Island. One day his father sent him to Singapore City, to sell pineapples.

"Go to the docks, where the big passenger ships come in," his father said. "People who have been at sea always like to buy fresh fruit when they come ashore."

So off went Lim Lin with his basket of fruit. The city was very big and crowded, and he didn't know the way to the docks. But he just headed to where the crowds were thickest and the noise noisiest. At last he could walk no farther, because of the crowd, and his ears were almost bursting from the noise.

He saw a big ship, and passengers coming down a gangway from it. But he couldn't get near them! He was jammed in the crowd.

Then he had an idea. He took a pineapple, and balanced it on his head. He put another on top of it. He asked a tall man to pile more pineapples on top of that!

Then Lim Lin began to walk, balancing the pineapples on his head. Everyone moved to let him pass. He walked all the way to the gangway without dropping a single pineapple. Everyone cheered. And they bought *all* the pineapples.

The Banana Boat

Omar was a boy who lived in Somalia, on the eastern coast of Africa. He lived on a banana plantation, near the sea.

Omar loved eating bananas. He also loved making boats from banana skins. He called them banana boats. One day he took a bunch of bananas to the seashore to make banana boats. He cut the side from each banana, being very careful not to cut the ends. Then, very carefully, he cut all the banana out of the skin, in pieces, making sure he didn't make any more cuts in the skin. He ate all the pieces. When the skin was empty, it looked like a little yellow boat.

When all the banana boats were ready, Omar tried to sail them on the sea.

Most of his boats were knocked about by the waves. They sank to the bottom of the sea and were never seen again.

But one of them was perfect. When the waves rushed at it, it just danced up their fronts and slid down their backs.

Omar stood on a sand dune and watched his perfect banana boat. He watched it sail out to sea, till it was so far away he couldn't see it any more. Omar waved it goodbye, and hoped it had a happy journey to some far off land.

Silly the Hippo

Right down at the bottom tip of Africa is the country called South Africa, ancient home of the hippopotami (hippos for short).

Once two hippos lived in a little lake in the middle of a grassy plain. One of them thought he was a very clever fellow, and he was called Smarty. The other one was always laughing and he was called Silly.

It hadn't rained for a long time. The grass was very dry, and the little lake had shrunk so much it was more like a big mud puddle.

Smarty didn't like it. "I wish it would rain," he said.

But Silly was staring at the sky. "Look at all the black clouds coming up," he cried. "I think it's going to rain now!"

They sat in their puddle and watched the clouds grow fat and dark. It started to thunder and lightning, but no rain came.

"I don't like the lightning," said Silly.

"Nonsense!" sneered Smarty. "It can't harm us at all." Just then a huge bolt of lightning struck the ground with a terrible crackle. Smarty was so scared he dived right to the bottom of the puddle and stayed there—until Silly dragged him up.

"Look, the lightning's set the grass on fire!" cried Silly. "There's no rain to put it out. It will eat all our grass!"

"We'd better run away!" said Smarty.

"We could carry water in our mouths, and pour it on the fire to put it out!" said Silly.

"Don't be silly, Silly," laughed Smarty. Whoever heard of a hippo putting out a fire? I'm off!" And he ran away.

But Silly scooped up a mouthful of water and ran and poured it on the fire. It only put out some of the fire, so Silly poured on more and more water. But the fire kept burning.

At last Silly got very angry—and an angry hippo is a very angry animal indeed! He rushed at the fire and stamped all over it with his great feet. He stamped so hard, so fast and so angrily, he put the fire out! And he didn't hurt his feet, because his skin was so thick he couldn't feel the fire.

Then Silly went back to his puddle. Pretty soon Smarty came back, and Silly told him what had happened. But Silly wouldn't let Smarty back into the puddle. "You'll have to find a new place of your own," he said. "There's not enough grass left for both of us to eat, and if it wasn't for me there wouldn't be any at all."

Well, Smarty went into a terrible hippo rage, but he had to admit Silly was right.

Now, whenever a hippo sees a fire, he rushes up and stamps on it. So if you're ever in hippo country, be careful where you light your campfire, or you might find a hippo treading in it!

The Leaping Elephant

Impala live in South West Africa. They have a truly amazing way of leaping when they run. They bound and bounce so high, they seem to have springs on their neat little feet.

One day a big elephant watched some impala leaping about. "My, they look pretty," he said. "I wish I could do that."

A passing secretary bird stopped in his tracks. "A leaping elephant would be something to see!" he croaked. "Why don't you try?"

"Don't be silly," said the elephant. "I'm too big and heavy to leap about."

"Come on, jumbo, let's see you jump!" taunted the secretary bird. "Or are you afraid?" He was really very naughty, don't you think, to tease the elephant like that?

By this time quite a crowd of animals had gathered to listen. They all stared at the elephant, wondering if he *was* afraid.

Poor elephant! What could he say?

He said: "I'll show you I'm not afraid. Stand back, everyone, I'm going to jump!"

All the animals scurried back. The elephant walked a long way off. He turned. He ran towards them. Faster and faster he sprinted! Then he bunched his great muscles and *leaped*! Oh, what an effort! Tons and tons of elephant hurtled into the air in a really magnificent bound.

And then he came down. CRUMP! Everything for miles around shook and swayed. The animals bounced as the earth trembled under them.

"Hooray! Hip-hip-hooray for the elephant's wonderful leap!" they cheered.

The elephant was very pleased with himself. "Didn't know I had it in me," he said.

"Squawk!" cried the secretary bird in a sudden rage. For the elephant's leap had shaken his big new nest down from a tree. The nest he had only *just* finished building too! Now he had to build it all over again! But it served him right, the naughty fellow.

106

SPAIN

A Tale from the Past

The magic carpet flew over Spain, carrying Fatima and Shamsuzzakir. Suddenly, the carpet spoke to them. It was a great surprise, for they didn't know it *could* speak! It said: "I am taking you on an adventure into the past. Someone needs your help. The answer is in the picture of the sheep and the flower."

"What answer?" they asked, but the carpet spoke no more. Suddenly it did a great loop in the air, with a funny little sideways jump at the end. Then it coasted to earth.

Fatima and Shamsuzzakir gasped when they looked round. The scenery they had been flying over had changed in an instant! Fields were now forests. Villages and towns and roads were gone. Rivers were in different places. Only the mountains looked the same. They were in the past!

They landed in a mountain pasture, where a young shepherd was tending a flock of sheep. His name was Manuel. They told him what the carpet had said. Then Shamsuzzakir asked him: "What help can we give you?"

Manuel stroked the beautiful carpet. "How clever it is, to know I have a big problem!" he said. "You see, I don't know when to take my sheep from the mountain pastures and move them to the valley for the winter. If I stay too long, the snows will catch us. If I go too soon, the sheep will eat all the valley grass before winter is over. When should I leave?"

Fatima and Shamsuzzakir didn't know the answer. They asked the carpet, but it would not speak again. Then they remembered what it had told them. They looked for a picture of a sheep and a flower, and found it right under their feet! It was woven into the magic carpet, and it showed a sheep running away from a pretty little star-shaped flower.

"I know that flower!" said Manuel. "Dozens of them grow right here, every autumn!"

They looked about. The little flowers were growing in the grass all round them.

"That's the answer to your problem!" cried Shamsuzzakir. "You must take your sheep to the valley as soon as those flowers bloom!"

So Fatima and Shamsuzzakir helped Manuel round up his sheep and herd them down the mountain. They were just in time! That night, a great storm came, and covered the mountain pastures deep in snow.

Manuel said he would call the little flowers *Quitameriendas*. That means: Flowers that take away the sheep's pasture. Then they all said goodbye, and the carpet brought Fatima and Shamsuzzakir back to today.

That adventure happened hundreds of years ago. But Spanish shepherds still call the little flowers by the same name. And they always leave the mountains when the little flowers bloom.

The Strange Catch

Aziz was a river fisherman in the Sudan. His river was a fast and furious one, in a great hurry to run down from the hills where it was born. Aziz fished in it with a big trap basket that was much taller than himself.

The basket was made of sticks, shaped like a cone. It had a wide round mouth at the top, and was pointed at the bottom. Aziz tied his great basket to the shore, on two long ropes. Then he put it on its side into the river, where the water rushed fast and deep. The water ran into the mouth and slipped out between the sticks. But the fish who came down with the water stayed caught in the bottom.

Fishing like that was very hard work. Aziz was always clambering about in the river. It was always trying to push him over and carry him away.

One day, when he was struggling in the river with his basket, he heard screams from the bank. A woman pointed to the water. "She fell in!" she cried. Suddenly, a little girl was washed into the basket. She hung on to the sticks and screamed too. If she let go of the sticks, she would be drowned at the bottom of the basket!

Aziz fought his way upstream, against the fierce current, till he was at the mouth of the basket. He reached in and caught her. But—*swoosh,* the river knocked him off his feet.

Now Aziz was in the basket too. But still holding the girl!

Oh, my! Aziz was very embarrassed. Fancy catching himself in his own trap! Then he thought it was very funny. What an odd pair of fish they were! So there, stuck in the roaring river, with a helpless child in his arms, Aziz began to laugh! The little girl was so surprised, she stopped crying.

Of course Aziz wasn't worried. He was a big, strong fellow. No matter how it tried, the river couldn't drown him, even if he *was* stuck in a basket! And while he guarded her, the river couldn't hurt the little girl, either.

When the mother saw they weren't hurt, she began to laugh, too. "Ho, ho, my fine fish," she called to them. "Don't swim away. I'll get some fishermen to pull you out."

She ran off and soon came back with a dozen strong men from the village. They quickly drew the basket ashore.

The woman picked up her child, very happy to have her back, safe and unharmed.

"What shall we do with this other big fish?" the men laughed, pointing to Aziz.

"With such a fine fish, we should have a big feast," they decided.

So they celebrated the rescue by having a big feast that evening. And the guest of honour was the fine big fish—Aziz!

SWAZILAND

Up and Down the Hill

In a little house, high on a hill in Swaziland, lived an old woman. In a burrow, in the side of the hill, lived a porcupine.

The woman tried to make friends with the porcupine. One day she set a dish of food beside her door for him.

The Porcupine *did* want to eat it! The old woman saw he was afraid. "I won't hurt you," she called. "Look, I'm going to the village. You can eat it while I'm gone."

Off she went, down the hill. The porcupine galloped up the hill and ate the food. Then he lay down in the sun and fell asleep!

Trudge, trudge! A strange sound woke him. Trudge, trudge! It was coming nearer! He jumped up and ran down the hill. Then he looked back. It was the old woman climbing the hill.

She called to him: "Do you like oranges?" She tipped her basket to show him, and two oranges fell out. Bump, bump! Down the hill they bounced, straight at the porcupine.

Did he run away? No, he did not! He liked oranges, and anyway he was very brave. But he did turn his back.

Bump, bump! They hit him—spoing, spoing! They caught on his sharp quills! He climbed up the hill with the oranges stuck on his back. The old woman pulled them off. She ate one, and he ate the other. Then they were good friends.

SWEDEN

Island Hopping

Stockholm is a fine big city, and the capital of Sweden. Between the city and the sea are thousands and thousands of islands where people have cottages for their holidays.

One summer day Sven and Hilda Nilsson were staying at their island cottage with their mother and father.

"I'm tired of fishing," said Sven.

"I'm tired of swimming," said Hilda.

"Why don't you take our little rowing boat and go island hopping?" said Mrs Nilsson.

Now, when Mrs Nilsson said island hopping she meant *rowing,* from one island to another.

But Sven and Hilda thought of a much better way to go island hopping. They couldn't really hop from one island to another. The islands are too far apart. So . . .

They rowed to the first small island. Then Hilda got out of the boat, and said "Ready, steady, go!" and began hopping across the island, as fast as she could hop. Meanwhile, Sven rowed *around* it, as fast as he could row. Hilda reached the far side first.

"I win!" she cried as Sven rowed up.

At the second island, Sven hopped and Hilda rowed. Sven won that race.

The third island was big. In the middle was Miss Gustavsson's cottage. Along came Hilda, hopping as fast as she could. She hopped through the front door, straight through the cottage, and out the back door! Miss Gustavsson was quite surprised at that, so she followed.

Hilda hopped down to the shore. Sven was already there. "I won that time!" he shouted. Then they rowed to the next island.

"That looks like a good game!" thought Miss Gustavsson, who soon saw what they were up to. She jumped in her boat and followed them.

As Sven hopped over the fourth island, he passed by Mr Hultin's house. A hedge was in his way; with a great leap he hopped over it. But he nearly landed on Mr Hultin, who was sitting on the grass. "Can't stop now!" cried Sven. "I'm island hopping!"

"What fun!" said Mr Hultin. He came hopping along behind. On the other side of the island, *two* rowboats were waiting.

"A race! A race!" cried Miss Gustavsson.

"Our boat against yours!" cried Hilda.

Sven jumped into his boat. Mr Hultin jumped into Miss Gustavsson's boat. They raced to the next island. Then there were *two* island hoppers, and *two* boats racing.

Lots of people saw them. "What a good game!" they all thought. *They* joined in.

Soon there were a dozen boats and a dozen hoppers spinning round and jumping over the island. What a wonderful game they had!

SWITZERLAND

The Skiing Goat

Switzerland is a small country full of big mountains. It's a wonderful place for skiing in the winter, when snow covers everything.

Franz was a wild goat who lived high on a mountain. He loved to watch the skiers playing in the snow. "I'd like to try that," he said to himself. "It looks like great fun."

So one day, while no one was watching, he stole a pair of skis. He carried them in his mouth, all the way up the mountain again. Then he stood on them—two feet on each ski. The skis started slowly down the mountain.

The skis went faster. "Whoa, slow down," Franz shouted. But the skis went faster.

"Ooooo," wailed Franz as they headed for some trees. "I'm, going to crash!" He closed his eyes. But, somehow or other, the skis passed through all the trees without hitting one!

Franz opened his eyes. "Hooray! I must be a wonderful skier!" he cheered himself.

Just then the skis shot right over a cliff! "Ohohohoh!" sobbed Franz as he fell. And he landed with a splodge in a deep drift of snow.

Franz scrambled out of the drift and shook the snow from his hair. "*That* was no fun," he said. He went back to the top of the mountain and never tried skiing again.

Farmer on the Roof

Fatima and Shamsuzzakir one day flew over the country of Syria on their magic carpet. They landed in a grove of mulberry trees, where the fruit was juicy and ripe. Soon they were both eating the lovely purple fruit.

Suddenly there was an angry farmer, rushing at them with a big stick in his hand!

The children were very frightened at that. They jumped on their carpet. "Fly! Fly!" cried Fatima. The carpet took off as fast as it could, but the farmer still managed to catch it by the edge! In a moment they were high above the trees, with the farmer clutching tight and screaming for help!

"Go down!" ordered Shamsuzzakir.

The carpet immediately dived down till the farmer landed on his feet. He let go of the carpet and it shot away, out of reach. Then they saw that the farmer had landed on the roof of a house. That was very awkward for him, because all the houses there had round, domed roofs.

The children told the carpet to go back and help him. But it was afraid he would try to hit them again, so it flew straight off, and never went back. And there on the roof the farmer stayed, till the villagers heard his cries and helped him down. No one else had seen the magic carpet, so no one believed his story of how he got there.

TANZANIA

The Fierce Rhino

In Tanzania, in East Africa, lived a fierce rhinoceros. He was a big rhino, with a fearsome horn sticking up from his nose. His eyes were mean and bad tempered. There was no peace for any creature who went near the fierce rhino. He chased every animal he saw. He even chased rhinos.

The land was very dry one summer, and the waterholes dried up completely. All the animals went on a long trek, looking for water. With them, snorting, chasing and making everyone miserable, came the fierce, bad tempered rhino. The sun burned down on the unhappy, thirsty animals.

Then a gazelle smelled water! he bounded away, with the others following. Soon they came to a waterhole, but they stopped. No one tried to drink. The fierce rhino came thundering up, pushing other animals out of his way. He didn't stop to see what was wrong, but plunged straight at the water— and got stuck in the mud!

You see, the waterhole had shrunk very much, because of the dry weather. All round it was deep, gluey mud. The fierce rhino was stuck fast in it. He thrashed and struggled, but only sank deeper.

The others grabbed his tail in their mouths and pulled and hauled and tugged. *Th-l-u-u-p*! The rhino came out of the mud.

A great hole was left in the mud where he had been. It filled with water, and everyone could reach it without getting stuck. They all had a good drink. The rhino was so grateful, he waited till last to take a drink, and didn't push or chase anyone.

You see, the fierce rhino had left something behind in the mud. It was his bad temper. He never got it back again, and everyone was much happier without it.

THAILAND

First Visit to Bangkok

In Thailand, in a village near the city of Bangkok, lived a young brother and sister. Their house stood on stilts in a bamboo grove. It was a very watery place, for the river called the Manam Chao Phya ran through there, in many channels.

Sometimes the children went to the rice fields with their father. Sometimes they went with their mother in a sampan to fish and gather water plants for food. Sometimes they sat on the back of their water buffalo as he grazed.

One day, they took a boat to the great city of Bangkok. The houses got closer together, and the canals became more and more crowded. When their boat could hardly move through the crowd of other boats, they went ashore.

The streets were thronged with brightly dressed people of many races. All around were shops, stalls and pedlars. The children stared at the fine gold and silver and jewels. They touched the rolls of soft, brightly coloured silks on the market stalls.

Then they saw a procession of men in bright yellow robes, carrying wooden bowls to collect the gifts of food people were giving them. They were Buddhist monks.

Then the children went to the new part of Bangkok where the old canals had been built over with roads. There they had a terrible fright. A great machine rushed past them, growling and honking! Of course, it was just a motor car. But it was the first they'd ever seen.

They ran away from it, not stopping until they reached the old canal again, and their boat.

And so they went home, after the greatest adventure of their young lives.

The Hidden Seals

Hasan was a young monk seal. He lived on the coast of Turkey, at the eastern end of the Mediterranean Sea. He could swim by himself and catch his own fish, but he was still much smaller than his mother, so she always stayed close by him.

They lived, with a few other seals, in a lonely cave at the bottom of a cliff. There was a small beach at the mouth of their cave, but no one else ever came to it. Hasan's mother never let him go very far from the cave. Whenever a boat appeared on the sea, she pushed and hustled him inside. One day he asked her why she did this. "I want to look at the boats," he said. "They're very pretty."

"Oh yes, boats look pretty and interesting," his mother agreed. "But they're very dangerous, for the fishermen are our enemies. They want all the fish in the sea for themselves. When they see a seal, they kill him."

Poor Hasan was frightened. He huddled at the back of the cave all day, and wouldn't go out even if there were no boats in sight.

Next day he did go out, to fish with his mother. Then they lay on the beach and watched the sea carefully. Hasan was afraid the fishermen would come back. Suddenly, he heard a strange noise behind him. He turned, and saw some unknown creatures climbing down the cliff.

His mother saw them too. "Men!" she screamed. "Jump in the sea! Swim for your life!" She splashed into the sea and swam away.

The men came towards Hasan. He had stayed where he was, too scared to move. A man spoke softly to him: "Don't be afraid, we won't hurt you. We're glad to see you, because we thought no seals were left here."

Hasan stayed, for there were many questions he wanted to ask the men. They told him they only wanted to help animals. They wanted to have strong laws made, to protect the seals from fishermen and hunters. Once there had been many seals along the Turkish coast, now there was just Hasan, Hasan's mother, and their friends, and a few others in the Black Sea, which is to the north of Turkey.

When the men had gone, Hasan's mother and the other seals came back, very glad to see that he was all right. He told them everything that had happened. But they were still very afraid of men, especially of fishermen and hunters.

Today, Hasan is still living in the same cave. He's waiting in hiding, hoping the seas will one day be safe, and seals can live at peace with men. One day, he hopes, he can go to visit his cousins in the Black Sea.

Deep in the Jungle

One day a little boy wandered into the jungle near his home in Southern Uganda. He lived near the Virunga volcanoes, in the middle of tropical Africa. The forest there grows thick and dark, and very soon he was lost.

He pushed through the jungle, calling for help, but no one seemed to hear him, for no one came. Weary and frightened, he sat and cried.

Suddenly, a great, hairy hand touched his shoulder. The boy turned—and what a fright he had. Standing behind him was a huge mountain gorilla! It was as tall as a man, but it must have weighed as much as three—and it was covered in thick black-brown fur.

For a moment, the boy was scared stiff. Then he remembered that gorillas are really gentle. They don't look it, but they are. All they ever want is to roam in peace through the jungle, eating fruit and plants.

Then the big gorilla took the boy by the hand and led him silently through the trees. After a while it stopped, and pointed. Just ahead was a clearing, and in it was the boy's house. The gorilla had brought him home!

Then, without a sound, the gorilla turned and in a moment vanished among the trees.

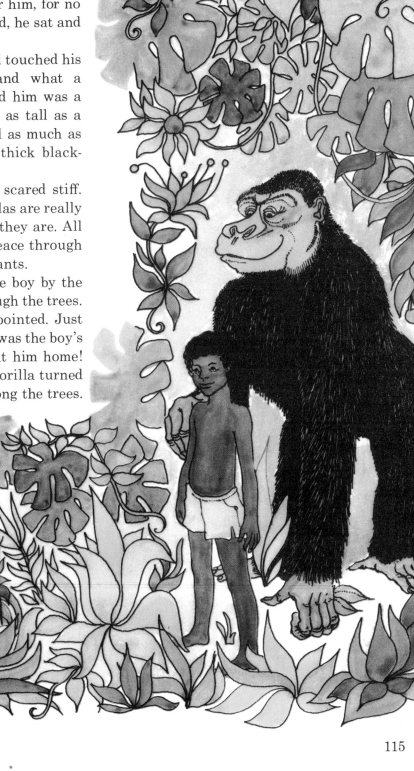

UNITED STATES

Possums on the Moon

Mamma Possum lived in a burrow in the ground with her nine baby possums. Her real name was *O*possum, but all her friends called her Mamma Possum. All day they stayed in the burrow. But at night, when the moon rose and coloured the wood a fine silvery-gold, out they came. Mamma Possum carried her nine babies on her back. They held on tight to her fur, and had a lovely ride. But, even better than riding, they loved the moon. They would sit and stare at it for hours.

One night, as they sat watching, a bright silver spark flashed across the sky. It was a space ship going to the moon! Suddenly, all the baby possums started crying, "Mamma, Mamma, take us for a ride to the moon!"

Well, Mamma Possum told them not to be so silly. "I can't jump that far," she said, "so how can I take you to the moon?"

But the baby possums cried and begged and gave Mamma Possum no peace. So she went home and wrote a letter to the president. It said: "Dear Mr President. Monkeys have flown in space ships. Dogs have flown in space ships. When are possums going to get a chance? My nine baby possums would like to go to the moon, and I wouldn't mind a little outing myself. So if you have room in your next space ship, please send us."

When the president read that letter, he was very surprised. "I didn't know possums could write," he said. "They must be very clever. Darn it, I *will* send 'em to the moon!"

So before you could say Sea of Tranquillity Mamma Possum and her nine baby possums were in a space ship heading for the moon!

They made a perfect landing in the middle of a flat crater. Then all the baby possums clambered on to Mamma Possum's back, and held on tight. She climbed from the ship and took a bit of a jump. Away they soared, and landed—plump!—in a drift of moondust.

"Wheeee!" squealed the baby possums. "Do that again, Mamma!" So she ran and jumped about on the moon till they were all quite covered in fine, glowing moondust.

Then they went into their space ship and flew back to Earth. What a fuss everyone made of them when they landed safely and came out of the ship. The president came to a party for them, and they had their photos taken. Everyone was very pleased with clever Mamma Possum and her babies.

Now they're all back home in their burrow, but they don't have to go outside to see the moon any more. Hanging from the ceiling are all their space helmets, still covered with moondust. They look just like one big moon and nine little moons hanging up there, shining on Mamma and her nine baby possums

The Gaucho

Uruguay, on the Atlantic coast of South America, is a vast, grassy plain of a country. On this plain, eating the rich grass, live thousands and thousands of cattle. The horsemen who herd them are gauchos.

Julio was a gaucho. He wore a bright shirt and a fine neck cloth, great baggy trousers and shining boots, and a big, black hat. Oh, he was a fine sight to see.

Across the wide prairies he rode, alone except for his horse and the cattle. One day he saw a wild horse dashing over the plain. It was the most beautiful horse Julio had ever seen, and he fell in love with it at once. The tame horse he was riding was a good horse, but the wild horse was ten times better!

"I must catch that wild horse," Julio thought. "I must tame him and make him my own."

He chased after the wild horse. At first it ran away, speeding like the wind, but it stopped and waited until he almost caught it. Then it ran away again. It was teasing Julio!

"Play games if you will," laughed the gaucho, "but you shall be mine in the end!"

After a long chase, the handsome wild horse galloped into a rocky valley. Julio rode after it. The tame horse stumbled, and fell, and Julio was hurled against the rocks. He struck his head and lay there, as if dead.

Frightened, his horse ran away. But the wild horse stayed. It licked Julio's face, and cried softly, and stood over him till he woke. Then it let Julio climb on its back, and it took him back to his camp.

You see, the handsome wild horse loved the dashing gaucho just as much as Julio loved it. So they stayed together, and roamed the great grasslands together, for the rest of their long, happy lives.

The Spectacled Bear

High in the mountains of Venezuela, in South America, lives the little spectacled bear. He doesn't actually wear glasses of course. He just *looks* as if he's wearing them!

He didn't always look like that. Once he was white, all over. That was long, long, ago. It was at the beginning of time, when all the animals were quite new.

They were very happy, being so new. They ran about the world jumping, rolling, dancing and playing for joy.

The little white bear was so excited, he ran round and round in circles. He became so dizzy he fell down smack in a puddle! "Ha, ha, ha, I don't care," he sang, splashing in the puddle. But he wasn't white any more. He was brown!

"Hey, hey!" cried the other animals. "Wash off that mud or you'll never get clean again!"

But the little bear was too happy to care very much. He just washed some of his face, leaving brown patches round his eyes. And the rest of him stayed brown, too.

And that's how the little spectacled bear got his spectacles. But do you know, he's still too happy to care very much!

The Monkey Hat

Flying over Vietnam on their magic carpet, Fatima and Shamsuzzakir saw something most strange. They saw a boy on a bicycle chasing a hat down the road. The hat was one of those pointed straw hats that Vietnamese people wear to keep their heads shaded from the sun. It was skimming along the road, ahead of the bicycle.

"Well, we've seen some strange sights on our travels round the world," said Shamsuzzakir. "But we've never seen a runaway hat before."

The hat hopped off the road, over a dyke, and into a flooded paddy field. It swam across, through the young rice plants.

"Oh, you naughty creature!" cried the boy. "Come out of the rice at once!"

"Ho!" said Shamsuzzakir suddenly. "That's not just a hat!" He steered the magic carpet low over the field. He leaned down, and snatched the hat.

Fatima lifted up the hat, and there was a little monkey! He had bunches of reddish fur on his cheeks and a collar of black and yellow fur. He was a langur monkey.

They flew back to the road and landed beside the boy. When he got over his surprise at the sight of them and their flying carpet, he thanked them for catching his monkey.

"He wanted my hat," he explained. "When I wouldn't give it to him, he ran away with it!"

Then he perched the monkey on his shoulder, tied his hat tightly under his chin, and rode off on his bicycle. He turned to wave goodbye as the magic carpet soared into the sky. The monkey waved too.

Dai's Dog

Dai had a sheep farm in North Wales, near Mount Snowdon. On his farm he had a big flock of sheep and one clever sheep dog.

One evening, Dai and his dog whistled and chased the sheep into their fold. Just as Dai was closing the gate, he felt a terrible pain in his back. "Oh, oh, this bad back of mine is starting again!" groaned poor old Dai. And he hobbled slowly home where Mrs Dai put him straight to bed with a hot water bottle.

Next morning, poor old Dai couldn't move from his bed. He called his dog to him. "You'll have to look after the sheep by yourself today," he said.

Dai's dog was very proud to be trusted with the sheep, all on his own. But when he reached the fold, not one sheep was there! The gate swung wide open. "Of course," said Dai's dog, "Dai must have forgotten to shut it last night, when his back began to hurt."

He ran all over the farm, but not a sheep could he see. What he *did* find was quite a strong, sheep-smelling trail, leading up into the mountains. Dai's dog followed it.

He tracked the scent for miles, higher and higher into the mountains. At last he knew where Dai's sheep were heading. They were climbing Mount Snowdon, the highest mountain in Wales!

"Silly sheep!" muttered Dai's dog. He ran all the way up Mount Snowdon. On the top were Dai's sheep, admiring the scenery.

"What *are* you doing?" growled Dai's dog.

"We've always wanted to climb Mount Snowdon," said the sheep. "Everybody does it. Lovely view, don't you think?"

Dai's dog agreed. Yes, it was a lovely view. Then he barked at the sheep, nipped their heels, and chased them back down the mountain again! He didn't stop till they were safely home.

And clever Dai's dog made sure the gate was closed this time!

Vana and the Volcano

Many years ago a beautiful woman named Vana lived on a West Indies island. She was the best cook in all those islands.

On the same island, a god lived in a volcano. One day, the breeze brought the smell of Vana's cooking to him. It was wonderful. He went down to find the cook, hoping she would give him something delicious to eat.

But when he saw Vana, he fell in love with her beauty. At once he said she must marry him, and come to live in his volcano.

Vana said no. She didn't want to live in a volcano. This made the god very angry. He put a magic spell on her that made her ugly, and she became so unhappy, she died.

Then the god was very sorry for what he had done, and very ashamed. He couldn't bring Vana back to life. But he put an everlasting spell on her grave. From it rose a plant, which climbed up and covered the trees with its beautiful blossoms. When the flowers fell, long seed pods grew on it. Soon people found that the pods had a delicious taste.

Today, plants like that still grow in the West Indies. Their flavouring is sent all over the world, so that everyone can enjoy it. The plants, named after Vana the beautiful cook, are vanilla orchids.

Assayed's Fortune

Long ago, in the land of Yemen, a boy named Assayed set out to find his fortune. His friends didn't want him to go. "Stay with us," they asked him. "We are poor, but that doesn't matter, because we're happy together."

But Assayed wouldn't stay. "I'm going to find my fortune," he said. So off he went, wandering through the Yemen. He travelled every road, and climbed every hill, and crossed every river but still he didn't find his fortune.

At last, he wandered so far he came to a place where there were no people. He was feeling very lonely when he met a crane bird, stumbling and hopping along the road.

"Why are you stumbling and hopping?" asked Assayed. "Why don't you fly?"

"I can't fly," said the crane, with unhappy tears in his eyes. "You see, I left my home and friends, to see the rest of the world. But on the way I hurt my wing, so now I must walk all the way home again." Then, with a pitiful sigh, he fell in a heap in the road!

Assayed was very sorry for the poor, tired, wounded bird. He picked him up in his arms. "I'll take you home," he promised.

It was a long way to the marsh where the crane bird lived. Assayed took two days to reach it, carrying the crane all the way.

When they arrived, all the other cranes danced for joy to see their long-lost friend again. They jumped high in the air. They threw sticks up and tried to catch them. They croaked and trumpeted and leapt and pranced. What a strange and wonderful sight they made!

Did you know cranes always dance like that when they're happy? They really do.

"How can we thank you?" they asked Assayed. "What do you want most in all the world?"

Assayed sighed. "I've been looking for a fortune for a long time," he said.

"*We* know where there's a fortune for you," hooted the birds. "Follow us!"

They led Assayed into the marsh, and showed him a rusty old chest, full of shining gold and glowing jewels! It was a treasure that had lain there, hidden, for many years. And no one knew of it but the birds!

Assayed thanked the birds. He gathered the treasure and took it to his home. Everyone was pleased to see his riches. But what really made them happy was having him home again!

Assayed was happy too, and he never wandered away from his home and friends again.

YUGOSLAVIA

The Fly-Foot Shoes

In Yugoslavia is an ancient town called Mostar. Centuries ago a strange boy lived there. He was always inventing odd things. Once, he invented a pair of fly-foot shoes!

No, he couldn't fly with them. But he could walk up walls and across ceilings, just like a fly! He showed off his shoes to everyone. He scampered up towers and over roof tops.

"Oh yes, very interesting," everyone said. "But what use are they?" Then they laughed and called him an idiot!

But one day, quite by surprise, the town was attacked by invaders from another country. All the men snatched up weapons and ran to the bridge over the river. There they fought like fury, to keep the invaders from crossing the bridge and getting into the town.

But the invaders were very strong, and the townsmen were soon losing the battle.

Then the strange boy had a very bright idea. He put on his fly-foot shoes. He crossed the bridge, upside down on the underside!

He came up behind the enemy, and gave them a surprise!

When two of the enemy chased him he ran straight up a wall and hung there, out of reach, making horrible faces.

Soon all the invaders were standing under the wall, gaping at the boy. He stuck straight out from the wall, held only by his fly-foot shoes. They forgot all about the battle!

The townsmen rushed up, grabbed the invaders, and threw them into the river. They floated away and were never seen again in Mostar.

Now of course the strange boy was a hero. And no one called him an idiot any more.

The Race

There once was in Zambia – which is in Africa – a farmer named Harold who loved horses. He thought about horses all day. He dreamed about horses all night. And he *never* stopped talking about horses.

One day, Harold was visiting his neighbour, Fred. Can you guess what he was talking about?

Yes, it was horses. Again.

Fred was bored to tears. He yawned.

Harold went on: "As I was saying, there's not an animal in the country that can beat my horse Lightning in a race."

Fred yawned again. Then he had a great idea! "My Ambler could beat him," he said.

"You must be joking," bragged Harold.

They agreed to meet next week, to race Ambler against Lightning.

Next week came, and so did all the neighbours. Everyone wanted to see the great race.

Harold rode Lightning up to the starting line. What a wonderful horse he was! His eyes flashed, his coat gleamed, and he pawed the ground.

Up shambled Ambler, with Fred just managing to cling to his back. Everyone laughed, for Ambler was a giraffe!

"What's this?" roared Harold angrily.

"This is my old pet giraffe, Ambler," replied Fred. "You said your horse could beat any animal in the country. You didn't say it had to be a horse! Let's see if he can beat my giraffe!"

Off they set, with Lightning galloping along, as smooth and beautiful a runner as you ever saw. Lolloping alongside, with Fred hanging on for dear life, came old Ambler.

It's no use trying to put reins on a giraffe, for his neck is too long. There's no way to put a saddle on his back, for it slopes too much. Fred rode bareback, and shouted his directions to Ambler. The old giraffe laid back his ears, stretched his enormous legs, and raced—very, very fast indeed.

He left Lightning miles behind, and won the race easily. For there's something most people don't know, and Harold never thought of. Giraffes can run far faster, and longer, than horses.

Poor Harold! He certainly learned his lesson. He stopped talking about horses, unless someone else brought up the subject first. And that wasn't very often!

Do you wish you had a magic carpet? It would be wonderful, wouldn't it? Maybe someday you'll be able to visit some of the places in this book anyway. And even if you can't go to all the countries in the world, you can always read about them— and that's almost as much fun as seeing them from the magic carpet!